"You did not see the man again?"

"I pray I do not see him again," Rosie stated.

"I will inquire about him in town," Ezra said.

"It is not your worry, Ezra. I am sure he left the area last night when we saw him drive past."

"As focused as he seemed to be to do you harm, Rosie, I do not think he will disappear so easily. Perhaps there is something you are not telling me. Are there secrets you must hide?"

"You need not burden yourself with my mistakes, Ezra. You have your own past with which to struggle."

Rosie thought of the rumors she'd heard about Ezra. For a period of time, he'd forsaken the Amish way and gotten caught up in the allure of the *Englisch*.

Something they shared in common.

Still, she did not want to discuss her own past with a man she hardly knew. Ezra had mentioned her secrets, yet undoubtedly, he had secrets of his own.

Debby Giusti is an award-winning Christian author who met and married her military husband at Fort Knox, Kentucky. Together they traveled the world, raised three wonderful children and have now settled in Atlanta, Georgia, where Debby spins tales of mystery and suspense that touch the heart and soul. Visit Debby online at debbygiusti.com, blog with her at seekerville. blogspot.com and craftieladiesofromance.blogspot.com, and email her at Debby@DebbyGiusti.com.

Books by Debby Giusti

Love Inspired Suspense

Amish Protectors

Amish Refuge
Undercover Amish
Amish Rescue
Amish Christmas Secrets

Military Investigations

The Agent's Secret Past
Stranded
Person of Interest
Plain Danger
Plain Truth

Visit the Author Profile page at Harlequin.com for more titles.

AMISH
CHRISTMAS
SECRETS

DEBBY GIUSTI

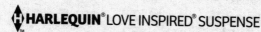

HARLEQUIN® LOVE INSPIRED® SUSPENSE

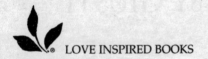

LOVE INSPIRED BOOKS

Recycling programs for this product may not exist in your area.

ISBN-13: 978-1-335-49066-7

Amish Christmas Secrets

Copyright © 2018 by Deborah W. Giusti

www.Harlequin.com

Printed in U.S.A.

Who hath delivered us from the power of darkness, and
hath translated us into the kingdom of his dear Son:

In whom we have redemption through his blood,
even the forgiveness of sins.
—Colossians 1:13-14

This book is dedicated to my wonderful readers.
Thank you for your support and encouragement.
You are the reason I write!

ONE

"Ach," Rosie Glick moaned as the December wind whipped the *kapp* from her head and sent it tumbling through the air. She stopped pedaling her bike, then propped it on the kickstand and ran to where the starched headgear had landed, only inches away from the steep drop-off that edged the North Georgia mountain road. She retrieved the *kapp* and brushed the dust from the stiff fabric, then glanced at the churning water, raging at the bottom of the ravine some twenty feet below. Her stomach roiled at the sharp downward slope and the bevy of boulders positioned along the sides of the incline.

Another gust of wind sent her scrambling back to her bike, all too aware of the growing darkness and encroaching storm. Rosie repositioned the *kapp* on her head and secured it with hairpins before she climbed on her bike, determined to get home before the sky opened and the rain commenced.

The nervous unease within her that had started in town continued to grow. She thought again of the man in the white sedan, talking on his cell phone. Pedaling past his parked car, she had noticed how much he resembled a person she had seen once and never wanted to see again.

Surely her eyes were playing tricks on her.

Thoughts of that horrific night rolled through her mind. The door to Will MacIntosh's trailer had pushed open, and the man with the gun had forced Will outside. Rosie had escaped, but she had not run fast enough.

Chilled by the memory, she glanced over her shoulder, relieved to find the road empty of vehicles. The last thing she wanted was to be followed. She felt sure the man in town had not seen her, yet she needed to be careful.

Datt would probably question her late arrival. He had never been a man of compassion, and since she had returned home seven months ago, he seemed increasingly short-tempered.

Even her sweet *Mamm* struggled with his behavior.

Regrettably, her father would never forgive Rosie for the mistake she had made. Baby Joseph was not the problem. Her own stubborn independence had gotten her in trouble, along with her desire to experience life to the fullest, even if it meant running away with an *Englischer*.

But Will MacIntosh had been murdered, and she had been trafficked and held captive for eight months. She had spent the last month of her confinement in a dank and dark root cellar where she had given birth to Joseph. The memory of their rescue and reunion with her parents had been bittersweet. If only her father had rejoiced at their homecoming.

Hearing the sound of a car engine, barely audible over the gusting wind, Rosie glanced over her shoulder. A white sedan raced down the hill.

She gasped and pedaled faster.

White automobiles were common among the *Englisch*, she told herself, hoping to calm her rapid pulse and thumping heart. Her legs burned from the exertion. The roar of the engine filled her ears.

The car's headlights illuminated the roadway, catching her in their glare. She inched as close to the edge of the road as possible and glanced back. Her heart stopped. The car was headed straight for her. She raised her hand to wave off the driver, but he continued on course.

The front wheel of her bike slipped off the pavement and onto the rocky berm. She lost balance and crashed to the ground. Pain ricocheted through her shoulders as she skidded across the hard-packed earth.

The car stopped. A door slammed. Before she could catch her breath and climb to her feet, the man she had seen in town was leaning over her. Dark brown hair with a long brushstroke of white near his left temple. Narrow eyes and a thin mouth. The same man who had come to Will's door sixteen months ago.

He grabbed her arm.

"Where is it?" he demanded. "Where's the information Will stole from me?"

She tried to pull free from his hold.

He slapped her face and twisted her arm. "Tell me."

She grimaced with pain.

"You were Will's girlfriend and his accomplice."

"What?"

"Don't act dumb. All this time, we didn't realize what he had taken until the last few days. When I saw you in town, it all became clear. He gave it to you for safekeeping, only we need it back."

Rosie tried to pull free. "I do not have anything you want."

"Don't act like a stupid Amish girl," he snarled. "You fooled us once, but you can't fool us again."

Tears burned her eyes.

"Will needed to be taught a lesson. Maybe you do, too." He reached for her throat.

"No!"

She clawed at his hands, which he had wrapped around her neck. Her lungs burned like fire. She tried to breathe.

Suddenly, as if hearing someone approach, he eased his hold and cocked his head. His eyes widened as he stood upright and stared for a long moment at the crest of the hill.

Gasping for air, she scooted to the edge of the incline. If only she could escape. But how?

Turning his gaze back to her, he grabbed her arm and pulled her to her feet. "You're coming with me."

The thought of being held captive again was too much to bear. She kicked his leg and gouged her fingers in his eyes.

"Aagh!" He dropped his head into his hands.

She turned to flee. He grabbed her shoulder. She jerked free, then tripped and fell to the ground.

"I need that information." He kicked her once, twice. Air whooshed from her lungs.

She rolled over and saw him raise his work boot again. Cringing, she anticipated the blow, until with one last thrust of his mud-covered boot, he pushed her over the edge of the cliff.

Her head hit a boulder. Prickly thistles and scrub brush scraped her hands and legs. Rocks battered her as she slipped and slid to the bottom on the steep ravine. "*Gott*, help me," she moaned until she no longer saw or heard anything.

Ezra Stoltz jiggled the reins and encouraged his mare over the crest of the hill. A car sat parked on the downward slope of the road. A tall man with a thick build stood in the glare of the car's headlights. He glanced Ezra's way, then quickly picked up a bike and hurled it over the edge of the roadway. Hurrying back to his car, he climbed behind the wheel, gunned the engine and headed north along the narrow country road.

With a flick of the reins, Ezra urged Bessie forward, the clip-clop of her hooves on the pavement in sync with his rapidly beating heart. Ezra had seen Rosie Glick pass the hardware store on her bike. With the fast-approaching storm, he had wanted to ensure she got home safely and had followed in his buggy. Seeing the man made him all the more concerned for her safety.

Nearing the spot where the car had parked, he pulled Bessie to a stop and jumped to the ground. Peering over the edge of the drop-off, he spied the bike, about ten yards below, and quickly descended to where it was lying.

He glanced at the steep downward slope and the boulders that pocked the hillside. Something near the rushing water caught his eye. He moved closer.

Blue fabric and a white *kapp*.

Rosie!

He scurried down the hill and kneeled beside her. His heart wrenched as he saw the blood that seeped from her forehead. Her arms were scraped, the hem of her dress torn. He touched her cheek.

"Can you hear me? It's Ezra Stoltz. Open your eyes, Rosie."

Ezra's heart stopped when she failed to respond. *Please, Gott, do not let another person die.*

Rose blinked her eyes open and gasped, seeing with blurred vision a man's face close to her own. "No," she cried.

His hand touched her shoulder. "You took a bad fall."

She shook her head, trying to identify the voice.

"I will take you home in my buggy."

Buggy? She blinked, noting his blond hair and blue eyes, which stared questioningly down at her.

"We went to school together. Remember me? Ezra Stoltz?"

Ezra? Not the man in the white car. She breathed out a sigh of relief and raised up on one arm.

The Ezra Stoltz she remembered had been tall and thin and nothing like the broad-shouldered man hovering over her.

He helped her sit up. "Are you dizzy? Does anything hurt?"

Her whole body ached. She touched the tender spot on her forehead.

He leaned closer. "It is a bad cut. You hit one of the rocks as you fell."

"Did you see what happened?" she asked.

"I saw a man on the side of the road. He tossed your bike down the ravine before he drove away."

She glanced up the hill. "Where is my bike?"

"I will put it in the buggy, but first, we must tend to your needs."

Grateful for his help, she tried to find something positive on which to focus. "I am scraped and bruised but not broken."

"This is something for which we can be thankful." He smiled, easing a bit of the fear that had tangled along her spine.

Helping her to her feet, he asked, "Are you able to climb the hill?"

"I—I think so."

"Lean on me," he suggested.

She had no choice but to accept his help. The incline was steep, and her legs felt like the congealed gelatin she made for her molded salads.

"Oh." Her knee nearly buckled under her.

"I will carry you."

Before she could decline his offer, Ezra lifted her effortlessly into his strong arms.

"I am too heavy," she said, embarrassed by his closeness.

He chuckled. "You are too light. Your *mamm* must not feed you enough. Hold on, and we will climb this hill together."

She wrapped her arm around his thick neck and dropped her cheek against his shoulder. Inhaling the masculine scent of him, she questioned her own good sense for allowing a man she barely knew to carry her in his arms.

As Ezra had mentioned, they had been in school together, but he was three years her senior, and she had seen him only a few times after he had completed the eighth level.

Once they reached the roadway, Ezra lifted her into the buggy. "Wait here a moment. Then Bessie and I will take you home."

Working quickly, he retrieved the bicycle and placed it in the rear of his buggy. "I can fix your bike," he assured her as he climbed into the seat next to her.

Grateful for his help, she relaxed ever so slightly. He lifted the reins into his hands and encouraged Bessie forward.

Ezra studied the road and then flicked his gaze to her as if to ensure she was all right. "Your mother will be happy when you are home, *yah*?"

Rosie rubbed her arms and lowered her gaze, thinking of her father's verbal attack and pointed questions.

"Thank you for your help, Ezra."

He nodded, perhaps as embarrassed as she was after carrying her in his arms. She brushed the dirt from her skirt and thought of the root cellar where she had been held captive.

She would not go back there. No matter what happened.

The clip-clop of Bessie's hooves soothed her frayed nerves, and she settled back in the seat, trying to think of what she could tell her parents when they saw the gash on her forehead and her scraped arms and soiled skirt.

Her own clumsiness and being too close to the road's edge would be truthful. She would not mention the man in the white car. Her mother worried about her well-being. The thought of being run off the road would be too much for *Mamm* to bear.

Lightning cut across the sky, startling Rosie. Rain pinged against the top of the buggy. The temperature dropped even more, and she shivered in the cold.

Through the steady downpour, she saw the headlights of an approaching vehicle in the distance.

Her heart thumped a warning.

"Do you see the lights?" she asked.

"*Yah.* You think it could be the man who threw your bike into the ravine?"

"Am I foolish to think he would return?"

"Not if you know the reason he wishes to do you harm."

Unwilling to share her past with Ezra, she sighed. "I—I am not certain."

He stared at her for a long moment.

"I was involved with the wrong person," she finally admitted. "It is too much to tell now, but that might be the reason."

Ezra flicked the reins and encouraged Bessie to increase her pace, which only troubled Rosie more. Instead of turning around in hopes of eluding the vehicle, Ezra was driving the buggy straight toward the approaching danger.

Fear gripped her anew. "Ezra, stop the buggy so I can run into the woods and hide."

He ignored her request and hurried the mare even more.

Lightning illuminated the sky and a crash of thunder sounded nearby. Bessie's ears raised. She snorted, no doubt skittish because of the storm.

"Please, Ezra." Rosie nudged his arm. "Stop the buggy."

The car was fast approaching. She could hear the roar of the engine just around the bend and could envision being caught in the oncoming glare of headlights.

She swallowed down the fear that clogged her throat and grabbed Ezra's hand, trying to make him realize the seriousness of her plight.

He pushed aside her hand.

Her heart crashed. Accepting a ride from Ezra had

been a bad decision. The boy she remembered from school was cocky, but always considerate of others.

She raised her voice. "Stop the buggy now, and let me out."

The glare of headlights preceded the car around the bend. She gasped, fearing the man from town would accost her again. Tears stung her eyes at the hopelessness of her situation.

Seemingly at the last possible moment, Ezra tugged the reins right. The mare turned onto a narrow dirt lane that angled off the main road. A canopy of tree branches brushed against the buggy's roof.

Rosie glanced at the road just as a white sedan raced past. Instead of being seen, Ezra had maneuvered the buggy into a hiding place that protected them both.

She let out a ragged breath.

Ezra leaned close, his face mere inches from hers. Concern filled his gaze and his voice was tight with emotion.

"Who is he, Rosie?" Ezra demanded. "Who is after you and why?"

TWO

"Take me home, Ezra."

"Who is after you, Rosie?" he again demanded.

"You have heard recently on the news of bikes being forced off the road and of Amish injured for no likely reason."

He nodded. "*Yah*, this I have heard. But those incidents were caused by unruly teenagers who wanted to make trouble. This white car was not driven by a teen."

"Did you see the driver?" Her tone was rife with defiance.

"Only from a distance when I first crested the hill. The windows of his car were tinted. With the failing light, I could see nothing when the vehicle passed by just now."

"Then you cannot say who was at the wheel."

He stared at her for a long moment. Rosie had been a determined young girl in school. She was even more so now. If only she would explain what had happened to her and why.

Ezra had no doubt that it involved Will MacIntosh, a known troublemaker who had convinced Rosie of his love. Will had gotten tied up in a number of schemes and died because of his involvement. Ezra had thought

Rosie was an innocent bystander, but now he wondered if she knew more than she was willing to reveal.

She started to climb down from the buggy.

"Where are you going?" He grabbed her arm. "I will take you home."

"You do not have to do this."

"You are in danger, Rosie. Accept my help."

She hesitated for a moment, then with a stiff sigh, she scooted back onto the seat next to him. "You are a generous man, Ezra."

He almost laughed. His father had called him confused and misguided. Even now, many in the Amish community were less than cordial when they passed in their buggies. Ezra had spent too much time associating with the *Englisch*, trying to find his way in life.

With a flick of the reins, he turned Bessie onto the main road. The temperature had dropped, and although the rain had eased, the damp air was chilling. Ezra grabbed a blanket off the back seat and wrapped it around Rosie's slender shoulders.

"I am not cold," she insisted, yet her shivering body revealed the truth. He did not mention her pale skin or the fatigue that even the darkness could not hide.

Under other circumstances, he would have lit the lanterns at the sides and rear of the buggy, but tonight, caution was important in case they needed to hide in the underbrush again.

Someone wanted to do Rosie harm.

Do not get involved, Ezra's voice of reason warned. The advice came too late. Whether he liked it or not, he was already involved.

Rosie and Ezra traveled in silence as the buggy meandered along the narrow mountain road. The closer they drew to her house, the more concerned she became about facing her father and anticipated his caustic words and demeaning gaze. If not for Joseph, she would run immediately upstairs and hole up in her room. But her child was the only spark of joy in her life, and she would not reduce the limited time she had with him. If only she did not have to work and could be with him throughout the day. Her father had recently demanded payment from her to cover the cost of food and shelter, which had left Rosie with no choice but to take employment in town.

"Thank you," she said to Ezra as her parents' home came into view. "You were very kind to bring me home."

"I will fix your bike and return it to you. I have much to do tonight, but day after tomorrow, it should be ready."

"Danke."

"I must return to town in the morning, so I will drive you to work."

His offer bought tears to her eyes. She glanced away, thankful for the darkness so he could not see her reaction.

"I do not want to take advantage of your thoughtfulness," she said, her voice filled with emotion that even she recognized.

"It is no trouble. What time do you start work?"

"At seven. It is too early, *yah*?"

"I will be at your house by six fifteen."

"I will be ready." She started to climb down and then hesitated. "The man who came after me has brown hair with a patch of white at his temple. He thinks I have something that belongs to him."

She hopped to the ground and ran toward her house. The front door opened and her *datt* stepped onto the porch.

"You are late," he grumbled.

"An older patient named Mr. Calhoun was in pain and needed help." She lowered her eyes and hurried past him. Before stepping inside, she paused and gazed back at the roadway.

Ezra glanced over his shoulder. Even from this distance, she could see the smile that played over his full lips.

Her father scowled. "Why does Ezra Stoltz bring you home?"

"I fell from my bike. He was good enough to help me."

"He is not someone with whom I want you to associate."

Her heart sank. Why was anything she ever wanted to do forbidden by her father?

"You remember what happened to his parents."

Their buggy shop had been robbed and his mother and father had been murdered during the break-in, but their tragic deaths had nothing to do with Ezra.

Rosie's father scowled even more. "Ezra was drinking at a bar in town that day instead of helping his father in his shop."

Which probably saved Ezra's life. He might have been killed, along with his parents, if he had been home. Not that she was willing to voice her objection to her father. Some battles were not worth fighting.

"He has not courted or taken a wife," her father continued. "Nor has he joined the church. This is not a man with whom I wish my daughter to associate."

Her heart ached at her father's bigotry. Did he not see the plank in his own eye?

"I am not looking for a husband, *Datt*." Her voice was firm.

"Joseph needs a father."

Rosie could not argue. Her son needed a father, but that did not mean she needed a husband.

She stepped into the kitchen, smelling the homemade bread and hearty beef stew her mother had served for the evening meal. Her mouth watered and she realized she had been busy helping patients all day and had failed to take either her lunch or her evening break.

Food could wait. She quickly washed her hands at the sink and then hurried to where her son sat playing on the floor. She raised Joseph into her arms and smothered him with kisses until he giggled and nuzzled her neck. He was eight months old with a happy disposition and a laugh that drove away any thought of her problems.

Rosie's heart soared. Nothing mattered except her child.

"*Ach*, what has happened?" Her mother's eyes were wide as she pointed to the scrapes and scratches on Rosie's face and hands.

"I fell from my bike."

"You have a bad cut to your forehead. Sit." She pointed to the kitchen table. "I saved a bowl of stew. You are hungry, *yah*?"

Holding Joseph in her left arm, Rosie slipped onto the bench at the table, bowed her head and offered a prayer of thanks for her safe return home before she eagerly lifted a heaping spoonful of stew to her mouth.

"After you eat and prepare Joseph for bed, then you will tell me what made you late coming home from work."

Her mother had a keen sixth sense. Rosie would be careful not to reveal what really had happened lest *Mamm* worry too much.

"The uneven pavement on the road caused me to fall, *Mamm*. I was not hurt."

"For this, I am glad, but the cut needs doctoring."

Her mother retrieved a first-aid kit from a kitchen cabinet and dampened a cloth that she wiped over Rosie's forehead. After cleaning the area, she applied ointment and covered the cut with a bandage.

"The town is decorated for Christmas, *yah*?" her mother asked as she returned the kit to the cabinet.

"Candy canes and snowmen hang from the street-lights." Rosie smiled. "Joseph would enjoy seeing the hanging lights and evergreen wreaths."

Although after what had happened today, Rosie did not want Joseph anywhere near town. She glanced at the end of the table, noting an envelope that had surely come in the mail.

In hopes of further distracting her mother from what had happened tonight, Rosie asked, "You received a Christmas card today?"

"From your cousin, Alice. She said baby Becca is growing and big sister Diane is almost as tall as their kitchen table."

"Diane is a sweet girl. I am glad you cared for her when Alice was on bed rest before Becca was born."

Mamm offered a weak smile. "She filled a void when you were gone."

The pain in her mother's eyes tore at Rosie's heart. She dropped her spoon into the bowl and scooted back from the table. *Mamm* rarely talked about that time when Rosie was held captive, for which she was grateful. Perhaps her mother's worry about Rosie arriving home late tonight had loosened her tongue.

"I will wash the dishes after I put Joseph to bed."

"No need to hurry, Rosie. There is only your bowl. I will have it washed and back in the cabinet before you return."

Rosie climbed the stairs with Joseph in her arms. She changed his diaper and dressed him in a fresh sleeper before they cuddled in the rocker. She crooned a lullaby as he nestled in her arms, her heart bursting with love for this sweet child.

His eyes drifted closed, but she continued to hold him, taking comfort from his precious closeness. His tiny hand clutched her finger, signaling their connection. Both of them had been through so much.

She thought back to Joseph's birth as she labored alone in the dark and damp root cellar. She had prayed her child would be born healthy and without complication. *Gott* had heard and answered her prayer. Somehow she had given birth to sweet Joseph, and for his first month of life, she had kept him warm and fed and secure in spite of their dire circumstances. Finally, they had been rescued and returned home.

The look on her father's face when he first saw them circled through her mind—it was one of relief, then shock when he noticed the baby in her arms. If not for her mother's heartfelt cries of joy and her warm embrace, Rosie might have run away again. The truth was she had no place to go and no one to give her and her son shelter.

She kissed Joseph's sweet cheek, laid him in his crib and covered him with a blanket.

Locking the door to the room they shared, she untucked the bottom edge of the quilt on her bed. Carefully, she worked her fingers along the stitched covering, and sighed when she felt the small toy and the money she had hidden there, both of which her father would not have approved. William had purchased the toy for their baby a few days after they learned Rosie was pregnant. She had secreted it away, knowing her father would not approve of anything William had given her.

Relieved that her secret hiding spot had not been discovered, Rosie slipped out of her torn dress and into her nightgown, but she was unwilling to go back downstairs. She did not have the energy to face her *datt's* questioning gaze or the concern she had seen earlier in her mother's eyes. Plus, she did not want to talk about her foolish mistake of falling for an *Englisch* man, which had caused her mother so much pain.

Rosie crawled into her narrow bed and extinguished the lamp. For these last seven months, since she and Joseph had been found, Rosie thought she had been safe, but the car tonight had run her off the road. The man demanded information Will had stolen.

Her stomach tightened. For her child's sake, she needed to find out what Will had done. When Joseph was older, he would want to know the truth about his father.

Her eyes had not fooled her today. The man with the streak of white hair was the same man she had seen at Will's trailer.

The man had killed the father of her child.

Now he was coming after her.

THREE

Ezra woke with a start the next morning and blinked, trying to distance himself from the dreams that had circled through his mind. He had tossed and turned all night as visions of a young Amish woman with golden hair and blue eyes disturbed his usually placid slumber. What was it about Rosie Glick that put him in such a state of flux?

With a heavy sigh, he rose from the bed, feeling confused and frustrated by the way his mind continued to focus on her troubled gaze that tugged at his heart. He poured cold water from the pitcher into the ceramic basin and washed with a vengeance as if to cleanse himself of any residual influence she might have on his life.

His father had called Ezra a dreamer who allowed thoughts of what could be to interfere with the reality of the present moment. Since his father's death, Ezra worked to remain in the present, which did not include a pretty woman with a troubled past.

With two hours of chores awaiting him, he hurried to the barn and was soon joined by his brothers, fifteen-year-old Aaron and eight-year-old David. Working rapidly, the three of them milked the cows, then fed and watered the livestock.

Inside the house, his two eldest sisters, Susan, seventeen, and Belinda, three years her junior, prepared breakfast. When the chores were finished and after washing at the pump, Ezra climbed the porch steps and pushed open the kitchen door, breathing in the rich aroma of fresh brewed coffee and homemade biscuits hot from the oven.

Susan turned from the wood-burning stove and greeted him with a smile as he wiped his boots on the rug and hung his hat on the wall peg.

His oldest sister cared for the four younger siblings, for which Ezra was grateful. Susan was pragmatic and task-oriented, not a dreamer like her older brother.

Seven-year-old Mary, blonde and blue-eyed, had gathered eggs from the henhouse earlier and now brought the cool milk and butter inside from the bucket, where they had remained overnight. Aaron and David followed her into the kitchen.

At one time before his parents' deaths, Ezra had thought of ways to get out of work. Now he focused on the farm and what needed to be done. The responsibility to feed and care for his siblings had fallen hard on his shoulders. If he had been less of a dreamer and more attentive to his parents, they might still be alive.

His five siblings gathered at the table and followed Ezra's lead as he bowed his head to pray. The others were oblivious to the struggle that plagued him. His own inciting role in his parents' deaths weighed him down like a giant millstone, as the Bible said, so that he had trouble offering thanks. At least his youngest brothers and sisters had been at school that day and away from the house. Perhaps that fact was the blessing on which he needed to focus.

Aaron had been working in the fields, and Susan had been at a quilting. If only their mother had gone with her.

He raised his head and reached for his fork, needing to redirect his thoughts. "Tell me, David, what you are learning at school?"

The boy looked pensive as he spread apple butter on a biscuit. "We learn our sums."

"And you mind the teacher?"

"*Yah*. Why would I not?"

Thankfully, David had not followed in Ezra's footsteps.

"You are going to town again today?" Susan asked.

He nodded. "I must take the buggy to the blacksmith. Something is wrong with the springs."

"If you opened *Datt*'s buggy shop we could check the springs ourselves," Aaron said. "It has been a year and four months, Ezra."

"Someday, Aaron, but not now."

"There are buggies in the shop near ready for sale," his brother persisted. "You helped *Datt*. You could finish the projects he began."

Aaron gave Ezra more credit than he deserved. "Perhaps after Christmas and into the New Year."

His brother shook his head. "In January, we will be cutting ice for the icehouse. Come February, you will have another excuse."

"Whether we open the shop this winter or not, I am still going to town." He turned to Susan. "Is there something you need?"

"Susan would like to go with you." David smiled impishly and reached for another biscuit.

"Davey, eat your breakfast and mind your mouth,"

Susan admonished. "It should be filled with food and not words that make no sense."

Evidently, Ezra was not the only one aware of Susan's interest in John Keim, the blacksmith's son.

"Bishop Hochstetler's wife has need of a schoolteacher next year since Katie Gingrich and Benny Trotter are courting," Belinda explained, sounding older than her years. "She says they will surely be married by the time school starts again."

Knowing his sister's long held desire to teach, Ezra forced back a smile. "Have you forgotten your sums, Belinda? You are fourteen."

"I soon will be fifteen and sixteen the following year. I would make a good teacher."

"I believe you would."

"The bishop's wife will search to find someone within the community," Belinda insisted. "A teaching job would provide income. This would be a *gut* thing."

"*Yah,* bringing money into the house would be *gut,* yet you are needed here. When your sixteenth year approaches, we can discuss this again."

Her enthusiasm faltered. "Susan cares for the family."

Ezra nodded. "Susan is getting older. She must think of her own future."

"Not long ago, you said she is to think of the family first and her future second."

Ezra had said exactly that, but since then, his heart had mellowed. Perhaps he was yearning for his own freedom. He pushed aside the thought. Regrettably, he had turned his back on his family once. He would not make that mistake again.

He ruffled David's hair with one hand and squeezed Mary's chubby cheek with the other, wishing the twinkle would return to her pretty eyes. She was too young to grieve so long.

Ezra pushed back from the table. "Breakfast was *gut*. Thank you, Susan and Belinda."

He smiled at his youngest sister, hoping to bring a smile to her lips. "And *danke*, Mary, for gathering the eggs. You, too, are a help to your sisters."

Mary nodded but refused to smile, bringing sadness to his heart. If only he could change the past.

With a heavy sigh, he stepped to the door, grabbed his hat and then glanced back at Susan. "Shall I tell John Keim you have a lovely voice and might accept a ride to the next youth singing?"

Her cheeks pinkened. "Tell him I send my greetings."

Ezra hurried to the barn and harnessed Bessie to the buggy. He would visit the blacksmith and talk to the blacksmith's son to determine if John had the makings of a good husband for his sister. Ezra was not ready to lose Susan's help, but he would not stand in her way to have a family of her own.

He thought of Rosie, trying to raise her son. From what Ezra knew about her father, Rosie was not receiving the support she needed. All the more reason for Ezra to help her in whatever way he could.

The road to the Glick farm angled downhill. Bessie's gait was sprightly, and both he and the mare enjoyed the brisk morning trot. Ezra would give Rosie a ride to work today. Tonight, if he got home early enough, he would fix her bike and deliver it to her home tomorrow.

He did not want her on the road alone until he asked questions in town about the big man in the white sedan. Ezra had not seen him before, although these days he did not go to town often. Earlier, before his parents' deaths, he had run with some of the *Englischers*. He remembered most of the people, but not the older man with the splash of white hair.

He did remember Will MacIntosh, but he would not mention his name to Rosie. She had been swayed by Will's handsome looks and lavish spending. Ezra had been caught in the deception of the world as well and had yearned for material possessions and the money to buy them.

He did not blame Rosie for leaving the Amish way for a time, but he did blame Will for taking advantage of her innocence.

Rosie woke before dawn and prepared to leave her house earlier than usual. She worried Ezra would forget his offer to give her a ride. If so, she would be forced to walk to town.

"You should stay home," her mother insisted.

"I am scheduled to work. Plus, it is payday. I must get my check."

"And what will they say about the cuts and scrapes to your face and hands?"

"I will tell them I fell from my bike just as I told you."

"Your father could take you in the buggy," her mother suggested.

Rosie shook her head. *Datt* would not agree to making the trip to town just so his daughter—a daughter he still had trouble accepting back into the family—could pick up her paycheck at an *Englisch* nursing home. Much as her father wanted Rosie to contribute to the financial needs of the family, he also struggled with her recent decision to seek employment in town.

"Another *Englischer* will catch her eye," her father had grumbled to her mother, and Rosie had overheard.

Forgiveness was the Amish way. Unfortunately, his daughter's mistakes were too hard to forgive.

She grabbed her black cape from the peg near the door, and after kissing Joseph, she hurried outside. Her father stood in the door of the barn and peered questioningly at her as she walked briskly toward the road.

Brave though she wanted to be, her heart pounded rapidly in her chest. If Ezra did not soon appear, she would have to make the trip on foot and would need to be on guard as she traveled along the roadway. Thankfully, the sound of horses' hooves alerted her to an approaching buggy. Her heart lurched. Not from fear but from a sense of thankfulness as she spied Bessie rounding the bend. Good to his word, Ezra had come to fetch her this morning.

Rosie stood at the edge of the pavement and waved as his buggy approached.

"Have you been waiting long?" he asked as he pulled the buggy to a stop.

"I just came from my house. Your timing is perfect."

Ezra reached for her hand and helped her into the seat next to him. The warmth from his body drove away the chill of the morning air.

"Your cape is not thick enough for such a cold day," he said.

Just as before, he reached for the blanket and wrapped it around her.

"Thank you, Ezra, for the blanket and for the ride, although I hate to take you from your farm."

"I need to be at the blacksmith's today and do some

other errands in town. So you have not taken me from what I had already planned to do."

Rosie had half hoped he was making a special trip to see her, but that thought would be prideful and would play into the comments her father sometimes muttered about her haughty heart. *Datt* did not realize being locked in a root cellar had left her anything but proud.

"You did not see the man again?" Ezra flicked the reins and hurried his mare along the road. The sun was rising, and the morning light cast a surreal glow over the mountain.

"I pray I do not see him again," Rosie stated as she tucked the blanket around her waist.

"I will inquire about him in town."

"It is not your worry, Ezra. Please do not add this burden to your daily tasks. I am sure he left the area last night when we saw him drive past."

Ezra glanced at her for a long moment before he turned his gaze back to the road. "As focused as he seemed to be to do you harm, Rosie, I do not think he will disappear so easily. Perhaps there is something you are not telling me."

He glanced at her again and asked, "Are there secrets you must hide?"

Her cheeks burned, but she held his gaze. "You need not burden yourself with my mistakes, Ezra. You have your own past with which to struggle."

His brow furrowed and his lips drew tight. He glanced back at the road, making her believe the rumors she had heard about Ezra were true. For a period of time, he had forsaken the Amish way and had gotten caught up in the allure of the *Englisch*.

It was something they had in common.

Still she did not want to discuss her own past with a man who had only yesterday acknowledged her for the first time since she had returned home.

"Let's talk of something other than the past," she suggested with a defiant shake of her head.

"Two months ago, I applied for the job at the nursing home," she shared, needing a neutral topic to fill the silence.

Ezra kept his gaze on the road as she chatted. He did not speak for far too long, as if lost in his own thoughts. Thankfully, his interest seemed to pique when she started to discuss Mr. Calhoun, the delightful older gentleman with whom she had formed a special bond at the nursing home.

"Last night his rheumatoid arthritis was causing him undue pain," Rosie said. "He asked for medication but none was given. Finally, I went to Nan Smith, the new night nurse. She promised to straighten out the confusion. Mr. Calhoun does not have a family, but he is such a kind man and appreciates anything I do for him."

"I am sure you brighten his day with your pretty smile."

Her pulse quickened, and she wondered if she had heard Ezra correctly. No one had ever said she had a pretty smile. She did not need compliments or flattery, yet hearing Ezra's comment and seeing the sincerity in his gaze brought a smile to her lips.

"You are generous with your words, especially for an Amish man."

"Amish men speak the truth, Rosie."

Her heart fluttered with the speed of a hummingbird drawing nectar from a blossom. In an effort to calm the rapid rhythm, she focused on Mr. Calhoun and their special relationship.

"Hopefully, the night nurse cleared up the pain-medicine problem so he got the rest he needed," she said, as they entered town.

The Christmas decorations added a festive charm to the morning, and in spite of everything that had happened, Rosie's spirits lifted. Ezra turned onto a side street and pulled Bessie to a stop in front of the nursing home.

The double doors were adorned with two large wreaths tied with shiny red bows. Potted pines, decorated with sparkling white lights and red bows, sat on each side of the double doors.

He pointed to the parking lot.

Rosie pulled her eyes from the twinkling lights and followed his gaze. Her euphoria vanished, replaced with dread as she spied a white sedan identical to the one that had tried to run her off the road yesterday.

"Stay with me," Ezra insisted. "Do not go to work today."

"Surely the car belongs to someone else. I will be all right, Ezra. You need not worry."

"The blacksmith's shop is on Sycamore Street off the square. If there is a problem, you can find me there."

She hurried inside and passed the Christmas tree decorated with gold and red bulbs. Hurrying along the hallway to the left, she rounded an arrangement of poinsettias that surrounded a Norfolk Island pine and stopped short. A man stood in the doorway of the manager's office. Thankfully, his back was to her, but the streak of white hair confirmed he was the same man who had attacked her last night.

The manager's voice filtered into the hallway. "Come on in, Larry, and close the door."

At least now, she knew his first name.

Had he found out where she worked and followed her here? Or was his presence a coincidence that had nothing to do with Rosie or her job? She would not wait to find out.

Turning down a side hallway, she hurried to the kitchen, located on the far wing, where she would hide out this morning, preparing the patients' trays. By the time breakfast was served, the man would be gone.

At least that was her hope.

Ezra tied Bessie to the hitching rail and entered the nursing home. Whether Rosie wanted his help or not, he needed to ensure she was all right.

He walked past the Christmas tree and turned down a nearby corridor to the right, where he was greeted with a bevy of activity as aides dressed in pastel-colored scrubs hurried from room to room, waking patients and getting them ready for the new day. He headed down one hall after another, but he could not find Rosie.

Stopping in the middle of the hallway, he glanced into a patient's room.

Someone came up behind him. "May I help you?"

Ezra turned to stare into the face of a middle-aged man with dark eyes and a receding hairline. He was big and bulky and appeared in good physical shape.

"Do you have a reason to be in Shady Manor?" the man demanded.

Ezra glanced at the name tag hanging from a lanyard around the man's neck. Bruce O'Donnell, Shady Manor Manager.

At the end of the hallway, he spied another man. The guy with the patch of white hair stood staring at both of them.

Ezra needed a reason to be on the nursing-home premises, without making mention of Rosie. Her favorite patient came to mind.

"I know it is early," Ezra said. "But I came into town this morning and wanted to see how Mr. Calhoun is doing."

"Are you kin?"

Ezra shook his head. "No, but he is a nice man who enjoys company. Could you direct me to his room?"

"Visiting hours begin at nine, after the patients have eaten breakfast." The manager pointed him toward the nearest exit.

Ezra wanted to find Rosie, but not when the man with the streak of white hair was watching his every move. He headed outside and pulled his buggy around the side of the building, where it would be less noticeable. Ezra would stand guard at the nursing home for as long as Rosie's assailant remained inside.

In less than thirty minutes, the big man left the care facility through a side door. He walked quickly across the parking lot, climbed into his car and drove off.

Ezra let out a lungful of pent-up air. Minutes later, Rosie ran outside. Her face was pale. Tears streamed from her blue eyes.

He grabbed her hand. "Did someone hurt you?"

"Oh, Ezra!"

He wrapped his arm around her shoulders and hurried her to the protection of the buggy. "Tell me what happened?"

"Mr. O'Donnell called me to his office. He is the manager of the nursing home. He—he claimed—"

Ezra rubbed her arms and waited as she struggled to catch her breath.

"Someone told him I was snooping around in patient records last night."

"I do not understand."

"It probably had to do with Mr. Calhoun. I had talked to the night nurse. She planned to check his chart, but I never looked at any of his records."

"Did you tell Mr. O'Donnell?"

"He would not listen. He said medication had been stolen, and..."

She hung her head. "He accused me of being a thief."

"This does not make sense. Are you sure you heard him correctly?"

Rosie nodded. "He fired me, Ezra. He refused to give me my back pay and mentioned calling the police." Her eyes widened. "I am frightened."

He wrapped his arms around her. "Do not be afraid, Rosie. You are safe now."

Only she was not safe, and the danger seemed to be getting closer.

She laid her head on his shoulder as the tears fell.

"Shh," Ezra soothed. Rosie was soft and warm and smelled like lavender. Everything within Ezra wanted to take away her pain and protect her from anyone attempting to do her harm. He pulled her even closer, wishing he could wipe away her tears.

"I wanted to say goodbye to Mr. Calhoun," she whispered. "But when I went into his room—"

"What happened?"

"Mr. Calhoun—" She glanced up. Sorrow filled her eyes. "Oh, Ezra. Mr. Calhoun is dead."

FOUR

Rosie's head swirled with confusion. Seeing Mr. Calhoun's body with a sheet draped over it had startled her. Foolishly, she had thought he was asleep. When she pulled aside the cloth, she realized her mistake.

His frozen gaze and white pallor had broken her heart. Unwilling to believe what she saw, Rosie had run to the nurses' station only to be told what she knew to be true.

Tears came again. She leaned into Ezra's embrace, feeling the strength of him. He rubbed her hand over her shoulder and clutched her even closer.

"Last night, he was fine," she gasped between sobs. "He was in pain, but his vitals were good. I promised him help. Nan assured me she would track down the missing medication."

"The nurse you spoke to, do you trust her?" Ezra asked.

"Why would I not? She is new to the home and eager to make changes for the better." Rosie sniffed and swiped her hand over her cheeks, in an attempt to wipe away her tears. "This is all so frightening. First the man chases after me, and now a patient—a *gut* man—dies, and I am called a thief."

"Perhaps we need to talk to the nurse. She might

provide information about Mr. Calhoun's physical condition, including any complications that may have occurred."

As much as Rosie wanted to remain in Ezra's arms, he was right. Nan could provide information about Mr. Calhoun's death.

"Nan left the nursing home shortly before I arrived this morning. She may have been with Mr. Calhoun when he died. That would bring me comfort if he had not suffered and slipped away peacefully."

"If that is indeed so."

Rosie stared at Ezra's questioning gaze. "You do not believe *Gott* called Mr. Calhoun home?"

"I am wondering if *Gott* had help."

Rosie widened her eyes. "You think foul play was involved?"

"I do not know, but one thing is certain, you need to talk to Nan. Do you know where she lives?"

"In a new area of homes on the far side of the mountain. She invited me to visit and gave me directions."

"I will take you there." Ezra glanced at the door to the nursing home. "We must hurry in case the manager has called the police, as he threatened to do."

Rosie's heart sank. If Mr. O'Donnell involved the police, she might be hauled in for questioning. Would they believe her or Mr. O'Donnell, a well-thought-of businessman within the community?

Surely Nan would provide information about Mr. Calhoun's death. Perhaps she would also shed light on why Rosie had been fired.

Ezra helped Rosie into the buggy and then climbed in next to her. He did not want to frighten her any more than she already was, but Rosie's world was spinning out of control. If Mr. O'Donnell filed criminal charges, she would have a hard time proving her innocence, especially if medication had, indeed, gone missing.

An innocent Amish woman was the perfect scapegoat. Rosie did not have the wherewithal to defend herself against slander. Plus, she had been involved with a man known to skirt the law when it served his advantage. The *Englisch* would never realize how a woman who longed for love could be blind to the truth about the man to whom she had given her heart.

To make matters worse, she had been kidnapped and held captive. A weaker woman never would have survived, but Rosie had endured the months of her pregnancy and had delivered her child in a root cellar all by herself. Ezra called that admirable and heroic, yet he doubted the local authorities would see her in a positive light.

Ezra encouraged his mare forward. Instead of taking the main road out of the nursing home, he circled to the rear of the parking lot and turned onto a backstreet.

"Does this lead to the mountain homes?" Rosie asked.

"*Yah*, it is a bit longer in distance, but it keeps us out of the downtown area. If the man with the streak of white hair is on the road, I do not want him to see you."

She lowered hear head and struggled to compose herself. He wrapped his arm around her shoulders and pulled her closer.

"After we talk to the nurse, I will take you home. We Amish do not talk about stress, but it is true that anxiety builds and rips us apart. You need time to heal."

"I need to find out what happed to Mr. Calhoun," she insisted.

"You also need to find out why the man with the patch of white hair is out to do you harm."

"His name is Larry. I overheard the nursing-home manager talking to him." Rosie wiped her hand over her cheeks. "I have so many questions. Perhaps learning about Mr. Calhoun's death will provide a few answers."

The community of newly constructed homes appeared on the distant hillside. "I remember when the mountains were covered with trees," Ezra mused, thinking of the changes that came with the increase in population. "The town grows too fast."

"Nan worked in one of the big medical centers in Atlanta. She wanted to enjoy a more rural way of life and moved here after she got the job at the nursing home."

Ezra glanced around the side of the buggy and studied the road.

"Do you see something?" Rosie asked.

"No one in a white car, if that is your concern. I saw Larry in the nursing home earlier. I went inside to ensure you were all right, but the manager told me to leave. I mentioned wanting to visit Mr. Calhoun. Perhaps that is the reason the manager told me to leave. He knew Mr. Calhoun was dead."

Rosie shivered.

"You are cold?" Ezra asked.

"Not cold. Just worried, especially since Mr. O'Donnell said he might call the police. What would they do to me, Ezra?"

"You have done nothing wrong." He glanced at her, hoping to see more clearly into her heart.

Ezra considered himself a good judge of character, yet he had been wrong about people in the past. He did not want to make a mistake when it came to Rosie.

"You have done nothing wrong," he said again. "This is right?"

She bristled. "Of course I have done nothing wrong."

Could he believe her? Ezra hoped so.

Hearing the suspicion in Ezra's voice, Rosie steeled her shoulders and pursed her lips, not willing to be undermined by a man who seemed supportive one minute and suspicious the next. She had revealed too much.

Earlier, she had appreciated his concern and the way he had offered comfort with his strong arms and his gentle, soothing voice. Since he had found her at the foot of the ravine, Ezra had been a rock in the midst of her chaos. Now she felt the exact opposite about him.

Ever since she had met William, her life had been anything but peaceful. The Amish way that she had loved during her youth had become confining and restrictive in her teen years. Was it William, with his free spirit, who had swayed her away from that which she knew?

She had been young and foolish. Everything that had happened—her capture and confinement—had changed her outlook. Now she had Joseph, her precious child, who gave meaning to her life. She had gained maturity through all the strife. Not the easiest way to grow up, but *Gott* knew what she needed.

Although sitting next to Ezra in his buggy after the death of a delightful gentleman had her questioning everything. She clasped her hands and kept her gaze on the mountain homes, unwilling to allow her emotions free rein.

"Nan told me her street is the second turn to the left."

Ezra encouraged his mare onto the street. The steady

pace of the horse's hooves sounded as they headed up the hill. The neighborhood sat quiet in the crisp morning air.

The stillness troubled Rosie.

"There is no activity," she said at last.

"The *Englisch* are at work, even the women," Ezra explained. "Children are at day care or in school."

"I hope Nan is home." Rosie noted the numbers on the mailboxes and pointed to a house on the left. "There. That is the house number she gave me."

Ezra turned his mare onto the driveway and got out of the buggy. He tied the reins to a tree and then helped Rosie climb down. All the while, he glanced around the area as if searching for anything suspect.

"You are worried?" Rosie asked.

"Not worried but cautious. As you mentioned, it is quiet here."

They hurried to the door. Rosie knocked then glanced down the street, following Ezra's lead. His concern added to Rosie's unrest. She rang the bell again.

Just before she was ready to return to the buggy, the door opened. A very sleepy Nan stood in the threshold, rubbing her eyes, her red hair disheveled. "Is everything all right, Rosie?"

"I am sorry to bother you. You were asleep?"

"Not yet. I was getting ready to go to bed." She glanced at Ezra and held out her hand. "I'm Nan Smith."

"Forgive me for not introducing you," Rosie said as the two people shook hands. "This is Ezra Stoltz. He agreed to drive me here. I came to find out about Mr. Calhoun."

"Come in," Nan said, opening the door wide.

Rosie and Ezra entered the foyer.

"I talked to one of the other nurses last night about

Mr. Calhoun's missing meds," Nan explained. "We couldn't find his OxyContin so I gave him a couple ibuprofen. I also called the pharmacy and left a message about the missing meds."

"Did the other nurse know what happened?" Rosie asked.

"She didn't seem concerned. I did a little investigating on my own and found Mr. Calhoun wasn't the only patient with missing medication."

"What do you mean?"

"What I mean is that Shady Manor has a problem. Many, if not most, of the patients had orders for strong opioid pain medication—hydrocodone or OxyContin— but when I searched the medication cart the meds were missing."

"Had they already been given out?"

"Not that I could tell. I didn't even know the opioids had been prescribed for many of the patients—patients who don't have significant pain. I left a memo for Mr. O'Donnell."

Nan's forthright sharing about what had transpired last night convinced Rosie the nurse had left work unaware of Mr. Calhoun's passing.

"Would either of you like coffee?" she asked as she ushered them into the living area. "I'll fix a fresh pot."

"Do not trouble yourself with coffee," Rosie insisted.

"It's no trouble." Nan pointed to the couch. An overstuffed chair sat nearby. "Sit here. The coffee will not take long to brew."

Rosie held up her hand in protest. "We can talk without coffee. There is something I must tell you."

Nan stepped closer. "Is something wrong?"

"Mr. Calhoun died this morning."

"Oh, no!" The nurse raised her hand to her throat. "I'm so sorry to hear that. He was in pain last night, but his symptoms weren't life-threatening."

"I went in his room to say goodbye—"

"Goodbye?" Nan narrowed her gaze. "Now I'm really confused. Are you leaving Shady Manor?"

"Mr. O'Donnell terminated my employment this morning. He said I had gotten involved in a situation beyond my job description. He also said I had tampered with patient medication and he threatened to notify the police."

"You're kidding."

"I wish I were. He told me to leave immediately. I could not leave without saying goodbye to Mr. Calhoun. When I entered his room, I knew something was wrong. The nurse said he had suffered a heart attack."

"Which may have occurred, although I don't recall any record of a heart condition." Nan shook her head. "He was such a nice man."

Rosie agreed. "He said I brightened his days, but the opposite was true. He was considerate of my situation and always encouraged me to work hard so I could someday become independent and take care of Joseph on my own. His words were always filled with kindness and concern. You know I would do nothing to cause him harm."

Nan rubbed Rosie's shoulder. "You were a friend he looked forward to seeing."

"But I do not understand what happened."

"I'm working later today, Rosie. I'll check his chart and see what it says. The coroner's report won't be back for days, but I'll talk to the staff and see if they know anything about his death."

"Will you be able to read the coroner's report?"

"Perhaps." She shrugged. "And I want to track down the reason his medication was missing as well as the pain meds for the other patients."

"Can you talk to the pharmacist and Mr. Calhoun's doctor?"

Nan nodded. "After I get some sleep. How will I let you know what I find out?"

Rosie glanced at Ezra.

"I will bring Rosie to your house in a day or two," he quickly suggested.

A warmth settled over Rosie. Once again, Ezra had come to her aid. "It will not be a problem?" she asked him.

He smiled. "Perhaps then we will be able to ease your concerns about Mr. Calhoun. It will not be a problem."

Rosie turned back to Nan. "We will see you either tomorrow or the day following to find out what you have learned."

She hesitated a moment as a thought surfaced. "Perhaps I am being foolish, yet I must say this anyway. If you would be so kind, do not mention my name to Mr. O'Donnell. He claimed I interfered with nursing duties last night. Perhaps he feels I was too demanding in my desire to help Mr. Calhoun. Keeping my name out of the situation might be a good idea."

Nan nodded. "You're probably being overly cautious, but I won't divulge your interest in Mr. Calhoun's death. Especially since Mr. O'Donnell accused you of wrongdoing." She patted Rosie's arm. "I do not want to get you in more trouble."

"Thank you, Nan."

The nurse glanced at the wall clock. "The pharmacy will open soon. I'll talk to the pharmacist before I get some sleep. I'm sure she can solve the problem about the missing meds. She may have information about Mr. Calhoun's other medical problems, too. Perhaps she'll let me know if he was prescribed any medication for his heart. I'll also mention my concern about the number of pain prescriptions that seem unnecessary."

Rosie was relieved, knowing Nan would get to the bottom of what was happening at Shady Manor. "By any chance, Nan, have you seen a middle-aged man with a streak of white hair at the home? His first name is Larry."

"That sounds like Larry Wagner. He was in Mr. O'Donnell's office the night before last. O'Donnell introduced us. Is he causing a problem?"

Rosie shrugged. "He thinks I have something that belongs to him, but he is mistaken."

"He seems harmless, Rosie. I wouldn't be too concerned."

But Rosie was concerned, although she would not burden Nan with details about who Larry Wagner really was. A friend of Mr. O'Donnell's who was out to do Rosie harm. She needed to be careful and cautious where Mr. Wagner was concerned.

Rosie squeezed the nurse's hand. "I appreciate your help."

"Like you, Rosie, I'll feel better once the mystery is solved."

After leaving the nurse's home, Rosie followed Ezra to the buggy. She stopped for a moment to peer down the mountain. Shady Manor was visible in the distance. What was happening there that had caused a sweet old man to die?

Nan had mentioned a mystery, which was exactly what Mr. Calhoun's death might prove to be. How did he die and why had his medication gone missing?

FIVE

As concerned as Ezra had been about Rosie at the nursing home, he was even more concerned now. Somehow by befriending Mr. Calhoun, she had gotten tangled up in a search for missing drugs.

The Amish tried to distance themselves from the *Englisch* world, but they read newspapers and stayed relatively current on issues that might have bearing on their own areas of the country. The drug epidemic that seemed rampant across the United States had touched the Amish community, leaving some of their youth addicted.

Will MacIntosh was involved with Larry Wagner. But what was the connection?

On the way home, Rosie kept her head turned away from Ezra. Was she weighing what Nan had said or was she thinking back to her time with Will?

"I keep wondering about the missing medication," Ezra said, finally voicing his concern. "We both know prescribed drugs can be illegally sold for profit. Larry Wagner shows up and drugs go missing. He believes you have information that Will took from him. If Larry is involved in a drug operation, could that mean Will was involved as well?"

Rosie straightened her spine. He could sense her displeasure even before she turned to stare at him, her eyes filled with accusation. "How can you think Will was involved with drugs?"

"I was merely asking a question."

She lowered her gaze and shook her head. "I do not know anything about what William did except that the man with the streak of white hair—"

Rosie hesitated. "Nan said his name was Larry Wagner."

Ezra nodded.

"Well, Mr. Wagner believes I have something that Will took from him."

"Drugs perhaps?"

She shrugged. "I had the feeling it was information."

"Something that would incriminate Wagner?"

"Maybe. That seems likely."

"Did Will give you any papers or files?"

She shook her head.

"What about pills? Or a wrapped container that could hold pills?"

"Nothing like that. He gave me a beaded necklace that broke the night he was killed."

"Did Wagner have something to do with your necklace breaking?"

She shook her head. "Mr. Wagner did not break the necklace."

Ezra waited for an explanation. Realizing she would provide no additional information, he turned his gaze back to the road. He did not want to unsettle Rosie more than she already was, but he needed to find out the truth about her relationship with Will.

"Did *he* break the necklace?" Ezra finally asked.

"He?"

"Will MacIntosh. Was he abusive?"

"No, of course not. It's just that…"

Again she hesitated.

"Just what, Rosie?"

"Ezra, please. Some things are not to be shared."

He pursed his lips and forced the frustration that welled within him to calm. Will was not the nicest of men and there was no telling what he had done to Rosie. A broken necklace could also symbolize a broken heart or a broken arm or a black eye. Had he been abusive that night, or told her to get out of his life even when she carried his child?

Ezra sighed. He was foolish to get involved with a woman who had given her heart to a dead man whose character could be embellished with time. Eventually, her memories of Will could become more grandiose than the reality of who he had been when alive.

Needing to focus on something more practical, Ezra clucked his tongue, encouraging his mare forward. He directed her along the back roads and away from town, but he was still worried about the man with the patch of white hair.

Ezra turned to glance back at the road they had just traveled. If they were followed, he had no idea where he and Rosie would hide. Last night, they had eluded Wagner by hiding in the woods. They were currently traveling on a road that butted up to fenced farm fields that offered no place to hide.

His chest constricted as he thought of the danger that could overtake them both. Driving Rosie directly home this morning would have been smarter than going to the nurse's house.

"You are worried we will be seen?" Rosie asked, as if reading his thoughts.

He nodded. "*Yah*, it would be easy to spot us on the open road. The fallow fields offer no protection."

"I have placed you in danger," she said, her voice low.

"Danger does not worry me, Rosie, but I am concerned about your safety. Wagner was talking to the manager of the nursing home. What if O'Donnell gave out your address?"

"You mean the address to my father's house?"

"That is exactly what I mean. The man could track you down."

"My father will not let him into our house. *Datt* will protect me."

Ezra nodded. "This is something for which you are certain?"

"*Yah*. My father would not let anyone harm me or take me from my home."

"What about before?" Ezra asked.

"William MacIntosh did not kidnap me, Ezra. I went with him of my own accord."

Because she loved him. Ezra knew that, yet he had half hoped Rosie would deny her feelings for Will.

They rode in silence, which only made Ezra more unsettled. Rosie was probably thinking of Will and mourning his death. Ezra wanted her to explain how she really felt, in case he had it wrong.

"Thank you for taking me to town and to Nan's house," Rosie said. "Thank you, also, for bringing me home. I have occupied too much of your time and must apologize."

"There is nothing for which to apologize. I told you I had work to do in town."

"Which you were not able to complete after I was fired."

"Do not be concerned about me. You have enough to worry about with your own safety and that of your son's as well."

The Glick home appeared ahead. Ezra glanced around the property in search of Rosie's father but failed to spot the older man. Mrs. Glick came outside, the baby in her arm. Even from this distance, the child saw Rosie and waved his hands in the air.

Ezra pulled on the reins. Before he could help Rosie down from the buggy, she was on the ground and heading to her son. Ezra watched her hurry toward the porch, feeling a sense of loss he had not expected.

Rosie stopped at the steps and turned, as if realizing he was watching her.

"Have you met my son?"

What? He shook his head.

She took the baby from her mother, kissed his cheek and then carried him back to the buggy. "Ezra, this is Joseph. His father was William MacIntosh, as you know. I made a mistake once, but I did nothing that would cause a man to come after me now. I have asked forgiveness from the bishop for my fickle heart, but I was not involved in anything illegal."

"I never thought you were."

Her lips lifted into a weak smile. "I am grateful for your help yesterday and today. There are few people who have reached out to me since I have returned home."

"Are you sure it is the people who would not help or is it that you have holed up on this farm without returning to the community you knew?"

She hesitated. "What about you, Ezra? Do you join

in the activities of the community or have you holed up on the mountain?"

"I have brothers and sisters who need my care."

"And I have a son who needs mine. Perhaps we are not that different. Again, thank you."

Before she could turn her back on him again, Ezra raised his hand. "I still have your bicycle."

"I will not return to town soon so do not worry yourself about something that would probably be an impossible task. Sometimes that which is broken cannot be fixed."

She hurried back to her house. Her mother had already gone inside. Rosie stopped on the porch and turned to watch him leave.

"Wave goodbye, Joseph." She took hold of the baby's hand and waved it in the air.

Ezra could not respond. Goodbye was not what he wanted to say. The word lodged in his throat and refused to be spoken. Instead he flipped the reins and encouraged his mare to turn back to the road that would take him away from Rosie Glick.

His leaving would be good for both of them. Rosie would remain with her troubled father and her mother, who always seemed fearful. The family would eke out an existence far from town and with only a few ways of interacting with the other Amish. They would remain distant, removed from the regular Amish community as if their daughter's mistake had taken away their desire to live life to the fullest. Were they so guilt-ridden by her mistake that they refused to enter back into life?

Ezra doubted their Amish neighbors would consider the Glicks's problems any more challenging than the problems other families had. Ezra could relate, as Rosie had mentioned. He had lived reclusively on the mountain and been unwilling to be baptized or involved in the social aspects of the Amish way. His sisters had suffered because of his closed outlook, but now he realized his mistake—he would give them the freedom they desired and needed.

Susan was of courting age. He would not stop her from falling in love and marrying and from making her own way in life. Belinda, when she was old enough, would make an excellent teacher, of this he was sure. He would not inhibit her desires any longer.

And the buggy shop? His brother would have to wait. Ezra was not ready to step back into the workshop where his parents had been murdered. Not yet. Perhaps in the future, although today as he left the Glick farm and traveled up the hill, he could not think of tomorrow, and it was too painful to think of the past, while focusing on the present only brought visions of Rosie to mind with her pretty blue eyes and blond hair.

He thought of her open expression and her willingness to reach out to an old man in a nursing home, as well as to give her heart to her son. But she had given her heart to someone else. To an *Englischer*. She loved him still, Ezra was sure.

Better that Ezra leave now before he think any more about Rosie. He would push her out of his mind, although he knew it would take time—time and effort, because saying goodbye to Rosie felt like a knife stabbing his heart.

Silly of him to have gotten invested so quickly, although looking back, Ezra realized Rosie had captured his interest years ago in school.

Now he feared if he stayed around her any longer, she might also capture his heart.

SIX

Rosie woke to the sound of a car engine. Her heart jumped to her throat, and she instinctively reached out her hand and touched the crib to ensure Joseph was still there.

The rise and fall of his chest comforted her until the pounding at the front door had her racing to the window. Pulling back the curtain, she looked down to see a light-colored SUV.

Was it white?

She blinked and rubbed her hand over her eyes, trying to wipe away the sleep and the dream she had about a certain Amish man with understanding eyes and a square jaw. Ezra was not the one pounding on her door.

She heard her father's footsteps as he scurried downstairs. "What is it you want?" he asked, raising his voice.

Garbled sounds floated up to her, as if an argument ensued, then she heard footsteps on the porch. If only she could see what was happening.

It sounded like a scuffle. She strained to see through the darkness until two forms took shape.

She gasped as she saw a man throwing punches at her father as he cowered in the cleared area at the front of the house. Heart in her throat, she turned again, to ensure Joseph was safe, then glanced back, seeing her father on the ground. The man towering over him was poised to strike again.

His fist pounded into her father's stomach. Even at this distance, she could hear *Datt* moan as he rolled into a ball, trying to protect himself.

"Don't tell me you forgot how to fight, Wayne?"

The assailant grabbed her father's shirt, yanked him to his feet and pummeled him again.

"No," her mother cried from below. *Mamm* ran to where her husband had dropped to the dirt again. "Leave him alone, Larry."

Larry? Larry Wagner? The man with the streak of white hair? How did *Mamm* know his name?

"Wayne tried to be tough in his youth, but deep down he was a coward then, and he still is a coward." Larry brushed his hands together before he looked at the house. His gaze fell on Rosie's bedroom window.

She stepped back, hoping he had not seen her.

"Where is she?" he demanded. "Where's Rosie?"

"She's gone, Larry. Now, leave us. You and your kind have caused us enough pain."

"You're lying, Emma."

She got into his face and pointed to his car. "Leave now and don't come back."

"I'll find her," he said as he brushed his pants legs and glanced at her father huddled on the ground. "If you weren't here, Emma, I'd finish him off. You know how I felt."

He looked at the house and shook his head. "Did you get what you wanted? I could have given you so much more."

"Leave, Larry. And do not return."

He climbed into the car, turned out of the drive and headed back toward town.

Rosie flew down the stairs and out the door to where her mother knelt, cradling her father.

"Help me get your *datt* to his feet," her mother said.

Rosie put her arm around her father's shoulders and helped him stand. He was woozy and wobbled on his feet, but with their encouragement, he slowly climbed the stairs and entered the house.

"We will take him to the bedroom," her mother said with no additional explanation of what had happened.

Rosie eased her father onto the bed and then hurried to draw water into a bowl and bring towels to clean his cuts and scrapes.

Her mother met her in the kitchen. "I will tend to your father. Go back to bed."

"I can help."

Her mother shook her head. "No. Return to your bed."

"But—"

"Do as I say, Rosie."

"It was my fault, *Mamm*. The man said he wanted me."

"And I told him you were gone. Do not go outside. He will not come into the house, and we must make sure he does not see you if he drives by again."

"I did this to you, and I am so sorry, but—"

She stared at her mother, knowing her own eyes were filled with question. "He called you Emma. How did he know your name?"

"Rosie, go to bed."

Her mother hurried back to the bedroom, closing the door behind her.

Rosie glanced out the window and looked at the spot

where her father had been accosted by the same man who wanted to do her harm.

What was happening to her life? She had experienced a few months of peace after being released from captivity and had been raising her son and healing from her own ordeal, but everything was happening again, only now everything was so much worse.

Her parents were in danger, yet there was something her mother had not revealed. She knew the man who had come after her—Larry Wagner, the man with the streak of white hair. How could that be?

One thing was certain, Rosie could no longer stay and bring more danger to her parents. She had done enough to cause them problems. She needed to leave in the morning.

But a sinking feeling settled in her stomach. She needed to leave but where would she go?

Sleep eluded Ezra. Every time he closed his eyes, he saw Rosie, brow furrowed and fear reflecting from her eyes. With a sigh, he turned to his side and rolled out of bed. He would not stay put when so much awaited him.

He glanced again out the window, relieved to see the first hint of morning light on the horizon. He would get an early start on the day. Surely Rosie rose early, just as everyone did in every Amish home. He envisioned her mixing flour for the breakfast biscuits and could almost smell them baking.

Realizing he was smelling the biscuits his sister Susan was making eased some of his angst. As always, he was grateful for her help and hurried downstairs.

"You are early for breakfast," Susan said.

Ezra reached around her and grabbed a warm biscuit from the baking sheet. "There is work to be done this morning."

"Yet, you were up late tinkering with a woman's bicycle. This belongs to someone you know?"

He bit into the biscuit and tasted its sweetness.

Susan turned from the stove and stared at him, her brow raised as if waiting for his reply.

He swallowed and smiled. "There is coffee?"

She took a cup from the cupboard and filled it with coffee from the pot. "I always have coffee ready in the morning. But you did not answer my question about the bike."

"It belongs to Rosie Glick."

His sister's eyes widened ever so slightly before she turned back to the stove. "The same Rosie Glick who was held captive for eight months?"

"I know of no other woman by that name in this area."

"I heard she works at the nursing home in town. This is who you have visited these last few days?"

"You are full of questions this morning, Susan."

"And you, my *bruder*, are hesitant to answer them."

She broke two eggs into a skillet. The hot grease sizzled. "Do you wish ham to go with your eggs?"

"Not this morning. I must leave soon."

"Before chores?"

"The boys can handle them today. I will return in an hour or so."

"You are delivering the bike?"

"Yah."

"Datt ran a buggy-making shop. Now you are working on bicycles. Is this a new venture?"

"I am helping a woman who has no one to help her. Surely this is something you can understand."

Once the eggs cooked, Susan used a spatula to lift them from the skillet. She arranged them on a plate, next to two more biscuits.

"You have a soft heart, Ezra, especially for those in need. This is a good attribute, *yah*? But you must use your head as well as your heart."

She smiled knowingly at him as she handed him the filled plate.

"I am not blind, Susan. I see clearly."

"Yet you still struggle to find your way and have not yet accepted baptism. Having this family to care for returned you to us, but I sense you do not know the direction with which you should walk into the future. We hold you back, perhaps. This woman might hold you back even more."

"I would think my staying here would be a good decision."

"*Yah*, in *my* mind it is the right decision. But we are talking about you, Ezra. You must decide what is best for you."

"Sometimes circumstances take that decision from a person. He no longer has the freedom to decide due to the responsibility placed on his shoulders."

"You are a strong man, Ezra. You can carry much weight, but you do not need added burdens that will weigh you down even more."

He scooped a forkful of eggs into his mouth and washed it down with coffee as she spoke.

"Rosie Glick is not a burden, Susan. I appreciate your concern for my well-being, but you need not worry. I know where I am going."

He hurriedly finished breakfast and headed to the barn to hitch Bessie to the buggy. The day was cold, but he appreciated the clearness of the air and welcomed the chance to leave his sister's watchful eye.

Susan was right. He did question his future, but his wanderlust had ebbed with the deaths of his parents. The Amish life that had initially held him back from experiencing the world now provided stability and a firm foundation on which to build his future, although he questioned where the future would take him.

He loved his brothers and sisters. He could not and would not abandon them again.

In spite of what Susan said, Ezra had his eyes wide open when it came to Rosie Glick. He would return the bike to her this morning and that would end their relationship. He had helped her to escape Larry Wagner. She had lost her job and planned to remain safely at home. Ezra no longer need worry about her.

But as the buggy left his house and headed down the mountain, Ezra knew the man with the patch of white hair was still a threat. He had come after Rosie once. He would surely come after her again.

SEVEN

Rosie left her house soon after the first light of the winter sun appeared over the horizon. She cradled Joseph close in her arms. On her back, she had tied a bundle of his clothing, extra blankets and diapers. She refused to disturb her parents, and instead of saying goodbye, she had left them a note on the kitchen table, explaining that she would contact them once she and Joseph were settled. Somewhere.

Today, she would walk to her Aunt Katherine's house. Katherine was her mother's sister, who lived higher up the mountain—her husband had died two years ago, and her daughter, Alice, had married and moved to Ohio a few years earlier. Katherine's son-in-law was a good carpenter, like her husband had been. Holmes County in Ohio was experiencing a tourist boom with much new construction. Hotels, shops and restaurants were springing up, bringing jobs that Alice's husband had quickly found in commercial construction. Perhaps Rosie could find a job there in one of the many stores or restaurants. But first, she needed to ensure she and Joseph were safe. If she holed up in her aunt's house for a day or two, the man after her might give up his search. Then she and Joseph could leave the North Georgia mountains and take a bus to Ohio without fear of being followed.

Rosie glanced down at her sleeping child, unwilling to think of what the future might hold. She needed to focus on today. Once they arrived at her aunt's house, Rosie could make plans for the next leg of their journey.

The air was cold to her cheeks. She pulled Joseph's blanket over his head to protect him from the morning chill. The temperature had dropped in the night and a shiver of concern traveled down her spine. She glanced back at her parents' home. A lump formed in her throat as she remembered when she had snuck out in the night to meet William. How naive she had been. And foolish.

At that time, she had been seeing life through the eyes of an immature girl, giddy with what she thought was love.

William had little love for her in his heart. He had more love for himself and his need to be the center of attention. Rosie doted over him like a fool, which somehow fed into his need to be accepted. His own father had been abusive and had little use for William.

They were alike in that way, a fact she had learned all too soon. Although she did not consider herself self-centered at the time. Looking back now, she saw the pain she had caused her parents because of her own desire to experience life beyond her small Amish world.

Now she was leaving home again, but this time to protect her parents, although she doubted they would consider her absence to be in consideration of their own well-being. Her mother doted over Joseph. Surely, *Mamm* would cry for his loss.

Rosie turned back to the road and walked with determined steps to the end of the driveway, holding her breath as if her parents could hear her in the still morning. Her heart was fragile, and with a little coaxing, she could easily be swayed to remain at home.

She shook her head, unwilling to acquiesce and wondered again about how Larry Wagner knew her parents. If he came to her home once, he could easily come again. She had to leave and find a safe haven for her child. Joseph did not need to be raised holed up in a farmhouse where love was hard to be found and an abusive man had beat up her father. The child deserved laughter and sunshine and friends with whom to romp over the grassy meadows. She would find a new home for them that was free from danger.

A sound echoed down the mountain, causing another chill to run down her spine. Not an automobile, for that she was thankful, but a steady rhythmic sound that made her pause and glance into the dense forest that edged the narrow roadway. The sound grew louder, yet was still unrecognizable. She shivered, knowing anyone or anything could be approaching.

Unwilling to remain in clear view, she pulled Joseph closer to her heart and skirted her way into the woods. Tree branches snagged her coat and scraped against her cheeks. She kept her hand protectively over Joseph, covering his precious face from the branches and bramble.

Once deep in the woods and protected by dense foliage, she stopped and turned to stare through the underbrush at the road. The sound intensified, causing her heart to pound harder in her chest.

The baby stirred in her arms. She patted Joseph and rocked the baby, hoping to soothe him back to sleep. His eyes opened as he stretched, his precious face wrinkled up like a prune. A very cute prune that would have made her smile if not for the seriousness of their situation.

She glanced at the road and the bend on the other side of the dense forest, hoping to spy whatever was approaching. Pulling in a deep breath, she waited and watched as a horse and buggy came into view. She almost laughed with relief.

A gasp escaped her lips when she recognized the very handsome man driving the buggy. Without forethought, she ran from the forest, arriving at the roadway as the buggy approached.

The driver pulled up sharply on the reins. The horse pranced to a stop.

"Ezra, what are you doing here?"

His gaze softened when he saw her. Then, as if fearing someone was following her, he glanced into the woods in the direction from which she had just come and again at the road in front of them.

"What's wrong, Rosie? Did something happen?"

She quickly filled him in as he climbed from the buggy and hurried to her side.

"You're running away from home?" he asked.

"I'm leaving to protect my parents. Larry Wagner came to our house last night. He beat up my father. Thankfully, Mr. Wagner left."

"He was looking for you?"

She nodded, ashamed of the danger she had brought to her parents. "But the strange thing is that he knew my parents' names. Even more confusing is that they knew his."

"You are sure it was Larry Wagner?"

She nodded.

"Did he see you?"

"No, but my mother forbid me to go outside lest he be spying as he drove by. She wants me to be a prisoner in my own house." Rosie shook her head. "I cannot do that, Ezra. It is not the way I choose to live."

"Where are you going?"

"To visit my aunt Katherine. She is a good woman. Her daughter, Alice, married and moved to Ohio. I am hoping Katherine will take Joseph and me into her house until I can find a way to get to Ohio."

"Are you talking about Katherine Runnals, who lives higher up the mountain?" Ezra asked.

Rosie nodded. "You know my aunt?"

"I do. The road uphill is steep in places. Carrying Joseph and the pack on your back would be difficult. Let me take you there in my buggy."

She nodded. "Again you have come to my aid at my moment of most need. *Yah*, I will gratefully accept your offer."

He helped her into the seat and climbed in next to her. He touched her hand. "You are cold. The morning air is damp."

He reached behind the seat and pulled out a blanket. He threw it around her legs and then pulled a smaller lap quilt out and wrapped it over her shoulders.

In the pale morning light, Rosie noticed the delicate stitches on the quilt, close and tight, and the straight rows that marked a steady hand well-accustomed to wielding a needle and thread.

"The covering is much too beautiful to be out in the elements, Ezra. This quilt deserves a special spot in your home."

"I have others in the house. This one was made for the buggy."

"Your mother did the stitching?"

He nodded. "My sisters helped cut the fabric and stitched the pieces together on the machine, but my mother did the quilting. She sat each night near the fire, the fabric stretched on a small free-standing frame my *datt* made for her. She would sit for hours with her needle going in and out of the fabric."

"Is that how you remember her?"

Ezra flicked the reins. The buggy jerked into motion. He scooted closer to her and glanced at Joseph, who had fallen back asleep. "He is a good baby?"

"*Yah*, he is a good baby."

She pulled him closer and turned her gaze to the road. Ezra had ignored her question about his mother. Rosie's comment had been too personal. She should not bring up topics that caused Ezra pain. Her own parents were very much alive, for that she was grateful, yet recalling the beating her father had taken last night convinced her all the more that leaving home was for the best no matter how much she would miss her mother.

Would she miss her father? She glanced down at Joseph, who looked like a mix of William and her own *datt*. The two men who had been in Rosie's life. Now one was dead and the other was bruised and battered because of her. She was a bad influence and brought trouble to those who knew her.

She flicked her gaze to Ezra. Her stomach tightened. She knew so little about the grown man sitting next to her, but she recalled all too well the handsome boy she had often peered at over the top of her schoolbooks. Ezra had seemed oblivious to Rosie's presence, yet she remembered the way he helped the younger children and ensured the wood-burning stove was stoked and the fire burning bright. The other boys paid it little notice unless the teacher called on them, yet Ezra was quick to add logs or rearrange the wood to enhance the output of heat.

He glanced at her and lifted his eyebrows. "Did you say something?"

"I did not speak my thoughts aloud, but I was recalling your last year at school. I had not seen you since then until you saved me after my tumble down the hill."

"I would call that more than a tumble." His smile warmed her. "Plus there were a number of times when I saw you, but you did not have eyes to see me."

She raised her brow and tilted her head. "Did I ignore you?"

"You were more interested in someone else."

Now she understood. Ezra had seen her with William. Her cheeks burned with embarrassment as she tried to recall any time she had ignored Ezra. "I apologize for being impolite."

He held up a hand. "Did I lead you to believe that you were less than polite?" He smiled. "Your attention was turned to someone else. I used to think William MacIntosh was a fortunate man."

Ezra's words took her aback. She did not know how to respond, and so she turned to gaze deeply into the forest, wishing she was witty and bright and could make conversation instead of wanting to crawl in the back of the buggy and hide.

Surely, Ezra was exaggerating to make her feel better. He was that kind of man, one that would do anything to help a woman in need.

Which she was.

Gratitude. Again, her heart filled as she thought of his timely intervention today and yesterday. She had thanked him more than once. She would not become a clanging gong, as scripture said. Better to seal her lips so she would not embarrass herself further.

Again she heard a sound that was hard to distinguish. This time, the sound came from farther below on the mountain.

Ezra must have noticed the sound as well. He tilted his ear and glanced around the side of the buggy.

"Someone comes."

"Another buggy?" she asked, suddenly not concerned with giving voice to her thoughts.

He listened more intently. "I do not hear horses' hooves on the pavement. I hear a motorized vehicle."

"A car?"

He nodded and glanced into the dense woods that skirted the roadway. "Surely there is a path we could take deeper into the forest."

Rosie followed his gaze, but she saw only the thick undergrowth that would catch on the buggy's wheels and prevent its progression.

"Stop and let me off."

"What?" His eyes widened.

"Joseph and I will hide in the woods. The buggy cannot go there, but we can."

"I won't let you go on your own."

She touched his hand. "Be practical. If it is the man with the patch of white hair—if it is Larry Wagner—we cannot let him find me. If I hide, you can remain in the buggy. It is doubtful that he would harm you. Once he has driven past, we will join you in the buggy again."

Ezra seemed hesitant, but as the sound of the engine grew louder, he nodded. "I will come to get you once he has passed. You will be all right?"

She nodded. "Joseph and I will be fine."

* * *

Ezra helped her down from the buggy and watched as she hurried into the woods. Then, he climbed back to his seat and encouraged Bessie forward just as a vehicle—a white SUV—rounded the bend.

The driver tooted his horn. Ezra steered his mare to the edge of the road and watched as the SUV, the same one that had run Rosie off the road, drove past.

Ezra glanced at the woods, wishing he could see Rosie, but then if he saw her, the man with the patch of white hair could as well.

The SUV braked to a stop and then backed up. The driver's door opened and Larry Wagner, tall and muscular with a streak of white hair, hurried toward the buggy. "I'm looking for the Runnals home. Can you give me directions?"

"Is that Majorie Runnals for whom you are looking?" Ezra asked.

"Not Marjorie. Her first name is Katherine. She lives around here, but I'm not sure where."

"There is someone by that name in town." Ezra scratched his jaw. "Although on second thought, that person's name might be Christine Reynolds. Could that be the woman for whom you are looking?"

The guy shook his head. "I told you I'm looking for Katherine Runnals's home. Don't you Amish stick together and know everyone in the area?"

"I do not know all the Amish in town. Perhaps that is where she lives."

"Thanks for your help," the man said, his tone sharp and laced with sarcasm. He hurried back to his car, made a U-turn and drove off.

As soon as the car disappeared from sight, Ezra climbed from the buggy and ran into the woods.

"Rosie?" He looked left and then right, trying to find her in the dense underbrush. "Where are you?"

Heart in his throat, he ran farther, calling her name over and over again. Why didn't she answer him?

He had been foolish to let her hide on her own. Although she was not alone. She had Joseph, a tiny baby who could not protect himself. Now both of them had disappeared, and Ezra was to blame. His parents were gone, now a beautiful woman. His sister had been right this morning. Ezra never should have gotten involved. He had tried to help Rosie, but he had caused her harm instead of making her life safer. If he had been a real man, he would have found an area to hide the buggy and would have stayed with her and her child.

"Rosie?" He was frantic. Fear for her well-being climbed his spine and made him want to scream with rage.

"Why, *Gott*?" he said aloud.

"Ezra?"

She was standing near a large pine tree, Joseph still in her arms. He ran to her, unable to voice his feelings. Instead he opened his arms and pulled her close.

"What happened?" she asked.

He shook his head, confused by the mix of emotions that had welled up within him.

"Was it Mr. Wagner?"

"Yah." Ezra nodded. "He wanted to know where your aunt lived."

She gasped. "You told him?"

"I would not do that. Come. We must hurry. You cannot go to Katherine's house."

"But I have nowhere else to go."

"*Yah*, you do." He grabbed her hand. "Hurry."

"Where are you taking me, Ezra?"

"I'm taking you to my house at the top of the mountain. We will be able to see the road and anyone who might approach the house. You will be safe there."

At least that was Ezra's hope.

EIGHT

Rosie feared not only for her parents' safety, but also for her aunt's. Suppose Larry Wagner found Katherine's house? He had physically attacked her father. Rosie cringed thinking of what he might do to her sweet aunt.

"I'm worried, Ezra," she said once they had returned to the buggy.

"I have five brothers and sisters who will keep watch on the road heading up the mountain, Rosie. No one arrives at our house without someone in the family seeing their approach. As I told you, you will be safe with us."

She stared into his eyes. "I know you will protect me as best you can, but right now, I am worried about Katherine. Even though you did not provide directions to her house, someone else might. There are so few families who live on this mountain, I doubt Katherine would be hard to find."

"Wagner turned around and was headed down the mountain, Rosie. More than likely, he was going back to town."

"He may be stopping at my parents' house again." She shook her head. "I do not think they would have mentioned Katherine to him so how did he know about her?"

"If he knows your parents, he might also know your aunt."

Another thought crossed her mind, and she cringed. "My employment paperwork at the nursing home." She grabbed Ezra's hand. "It asked for information about my next of kin and had a space for another point of contact. I filled Katherine's name into that blank. A contact phone number was requested, which she does not have. Thankfully, the form did not ask for an address."

"So if O'Donnell shared your information with Wagner, he would know about Katherine. These two men must be working together, but you cannot blame yourself, Rosie. How would you have known that the information on your employment application could get into the wrong hands?"

"I have to see Katherine. I will not be at peace unless I make sure she is safe. Plus she needs to know about Larry Wagner. Perhaps she could leave the area and visit her daughter over Christmas to remain safe."

"How terrible that we would think someone would hurt a woman, yet after what Wagner did to you, there is no telling what might befall her. You are being prudent and wise to want to ensure Katherine remains safe."

Ezra grabbed the reins. "My father built buggies, as you probably know."

She nodded.

"When his work was done and he was ready to deliver a buggy to the buyer, *Datt* would do a test ride. He made a path around our farm. It runs above your aunt's home. We can look down on it and hopefully stay out of sight in case the man is there."

"We can do that now?" she asked.

Ezra nodded. "The turnoff that will take us to the

path is not far. It would be a wise choice to keep you safe as well. If the man returns this way, you might have to hide in the woods again, which is not something I want to have happen. By taking the path, we will stay off the main road and out of sight."

He flicked the reins and pointed in the distance. "The turnoff is not far."

Joseph stirred in Rosie's arms. To quiet the baby, she softly crooned a lullaby and smiled when he fell back to sleep.

"You sing like a songbird," Ezra said.

Embarrassed by the compliment, she kept her eyes on Joseph.

"My words bother you?" Ezra asked.

"I could never be bothered by nice things you might tell me, but I do not wish to be prideful."

"I doubt you could be that, Rosie. Besides, it is important to recognize your own gifts from *Gott* and thank him for them."

"I do that, Ezra, but I do not recall anyone paying me compliments. My mother wanted me to be free of prideful thoughts. She thought compliments were frivolous. I was to accept who I was and not wish for more than what *Gott* had given me."

"And your father?"

"I am not sure how he felt. He was not one to express his feelings, except if I did something that brought his disapproval, which I hate to admit was more often than I would have liked."

She adjusted the blanket around her sleeping child. "Even his gaze was often filled with accusation, as if he was waiting for me to make a mistake. I tried to be a dutiful daughter, yet I failed frequently."

Ezra shook his head with regret. "Amish fathers are the heads of their families, and they usually take delight in their children. I am sorry you did not have a better life growing up."

"But it was the only life I knew, Ezra, so how could I say that it was bad? It was what it was."

"Yet you did not feel love."

She glanced away, trying to sort through the mix of feelings. Had she felt love from her parents?

"Perhaps that is what I was searching for all my life."

She had made the wrong decision concerning William, she refused to add. Humiliation washed over her as she thought of the extent of her mistakes and the errors of her ways. She had turned from all she had been taught and run after a man who had promised her so much. Truth be known, the pretty jewelry and things of the world were not what she had sought. Instead it had been love, only she had learned too late that what William wanted to give her was not love…anything but.

"Did you ever make a mistake that you wish you could change, Ezra, yet if you did, that which is most precious to you would have to be given away as well?"

She glanced down at her sleeping child, who had been the good brought from her foolishness. She would do nothing to change her life as his mother. Surely that would be hard for a practical man like Ezra to understand.

She sighed. "You have made me share more than you wanted or needed to hear. Have you this effect on other women who accept rides in your buggy?"

"If by other women, you mean my sisters, I would say they are more than willing to share what is on their minds, even when I do not want to hear it all. They are strong women, perhaps too strong." He laughed. "I wonder if there will be any man determined enough to accept my fourteen-year-old sister into his heart. Belinda is forthright and speaks her mind whenever she chooses."

"An Amish wife should stand next to her husband but never in front of him." Rosie intoned the saying she had heard often within the Amish community.

Ezra smiled. "It was something my own mother said, along with the phrase 'equally yoked,' which she claimed referred to the balance between husband and wife, both working together and in step as they went through life and raised their family."

"My mother did not walk next to my father," Rosie said. "She walked behind him."

Glancing at the passing countryside, Rosie wondered why she was sharing so much with Ezra. She did not want to disrespect her mother, although she questioned how telling the truth could be disrespectful. Still, there was something about Ezra that made her lower the barriers she usually had in place. A mistake on her part, no doubt. She wanted to trust him, but she had trusted the wrong man before and did not want to make a similar mistake again.

"The turnoff is just ahead." Ezra glanced back, checking the road they had traveled. "Even though I am sure Larry Wagner is heading to town, taking the back path is still a wise choice. There is a northern access to the mountain, and he could come around that way, although it is doubtful."

"I am worried about Katherine."

"We will pass on the hill above your aunt's house and will be able to see if a car is in her driveway."

"And if the white SUV is there? What will we do then, Ezra?"

"We will decide what to do when and if we see his car."

"If I had gone to Katherine's house—" Rosie pulled in a deep breath and glanced down at Joseph.

"You are thinking of that which has not happened. Beside, you are not with Katherine." He smiled. "You are here in the buggy with me."

She adjusted the blanket around her baby and nodded. "Yes, I am with you."

Ezra chuckled. "From the struggle I hear in your voice, this is not a good thing?"

She glanced at him and laughed.

His heart leaped in his chest at the sound, then abruptly, he turned his gaze back to the path, startled by his reaction and unsure of the mix of emotions that were playing havoc with him. How could her laughter cause him such confusion?

Rosie seemed unaware of the effect she was having on him.

"The mountain is beautiful," she said, staring into the distance. "I have not taken the time to notice how tall the trees are here. Farther down the mountain, where I live, the land is more for farming. Trees have been removed and the ground cultivated for planting. I wish there were more rustic areas like this where I live."

Ezra looked anew at the forest that surrounded them. "My father, brothers and I would hunt near here and come home with fresh meat for my mother to cure and eventually serve. Our hunting trips were good memories I think too rarely about these days."

He smiled ruefully, recalling the jovial mood his father would be in whenever he and the boys hunted. "It is good for a man to be with nature. I must explore the forests more often myself."

Rosie pulled the blanket around Joseph.

"You are cold?" Ezra asked.

"A little."

"It is always cooler in the wooded areas. We are almost to the ridgeline, where we will leave the heavy tree cover and emerge into the sunlight."

"And will we see my aunt's house?"

"*Yah*, soon."

"I am worried, Ezra."

"But your worry does not change whether the man is with your aunt or not. My mother used to say that we will cross that bridge when we come to it."

"My mother said the same." She glanced down. "I will probably say it to Joseph, as well."

"We humans allow worry and fear to have dominance in our lives."

She tilted her head. "I would not think you worry about anything, Ezra. You seem assured of where you stand in life."

Rosie did not realize what he carried within his heart and the weight that had settled on his shoulders a year and four months ago, a weight that would stay with him throughout his life.

"There." He pointed to a small white house, nestled on the hillside. "That is the house for which the man was searching."

"Aunt Katherine's house." Rosie smiled. "We visited often when I was young."

"She is a good woman. Katherine and my mother were friends."

"Then go to her house, Ezra. Talk to her. Tell her to beware of the man with the streak of white hair."

He looked at Rosie for a long moment. "You could tell her yourself."

"And if Mr. Wagner comes to her house, what will she do? She would not want to lie and might reveal where I am. You go, but do not mention that I will be staying at your house." Rosie touched his arm. "Please. For me."

Her eyes were so blue, and her hand, gripping his arm, made his chest tighten. What was it about this woman that had such an effect on him?

He pulled the buggy into a cluster of pine trees situated near an abandoned barn. "I will do as you ask. Stay here, Rosie. No one can see you from the road."

"Be careful, Ezra."

"I will return soon." He jumped to the ground and started down the hill. Halfway to the house, he glanced back. Rosie had climbed from the buggy and was peering around the side of the old barn. His heart jolted as their eyes connected for one long moment before he turned back to the path and hurried toward the house.

Rosie was taking over his life. Too quickly. Two days ago he had been his own man, then he had seen her ride past the hardware store. Something had snapped in him, bringing back all the memories of their time together in the schoolhouse. Rosie had never shown interest in him and probably thought of Ezra as merely an older boy who struggled with being Amish.

What had been wrong with him then?

Something was wrong with him now, but it did not involve his upset with the Amish way. It had to do with a pretty girl with big eyes who was too serious. Why would Ezra be interested in such a woman?

He did not know why. All he knew was that he was interested—very interested—in Rosie.

Joseph's eyes blinked open. Rosie smiled at her baby and lifted the little one onto her shoulder. "Do not fuss, Joseph. We need to be quiet while we are close to Aunt Katherine's house. She could be in danger, and Ezra is warning her."

The baby cooed and chewed on his hand. Rosie rocked him back and forth to keep the baby happy, and all the while her gaze was on Ezra, now standing on Katherine's back porch.

He knocked on the door a number of times and then hurried around to the front of the house.

Was Katherine not home?

As Rosie waited for Ezra to reappear, she noticed movement on the road below. Her heart stopped. The white SUV was heading up the mountain.

She glanced at her aunt's house, searching for Ezra. He must be oblivious to the danger that approached.

Joseph whined. She patted and rocked and shushed the baby. "You need to be very quiet."

The little one tugged a strand of hair free from her bun and put it in his mouth. "Oh, sweet baby, that is not good for you to eat."

Rosie pulled her hair from his reach, hoping it would not cause an outburst from Joseph and somehow alert Wagner.

The car continued up the hill.

Where was Ezra?

The palms of her hands were wet. She wiped them on her skirt.

The baby started to fuss. "Shhh, Joseph."

Vulnerable and exposed, Rosie's pulse raced as she watched the SUV turn into Katherine's drive.

She had to do something to protect her baby, but where could she hide to keep Joseph safe?

NINE

Holding Joseph with one hand, Rosie grabbed the reins and guided the mare and buggy into the dilapidated barn. She pushed the door closed and peered through a crack in the wall of the old structure.

Mr. Wagner climbed from his SUV. He slammed the door, sending a jolt to her heart. With quick, determined steps, he walked to Katherine's back door and knocked. When no one answered, he put his hands on his hips and turned to stare at the hillside. He shrugged his broad shoulders, left the porch and climbed the hill, heading straight to where Rosie and Joseph were hiding.

Her heart pounded nearly out of her chest. She rocked the baby and held the reins with her other hand, needing both Joseph and Bessie to remain quiet. One cry from Joseph or a flick of Bessie's tail could alert Wagner to their whereabouts.

He approached the barn. Rosie held her breath. *Please, Gott, protect us.*

Joseph stretched his arms and sighed.

She froze, fearing Wagner had heard.

Rosie peered through the slats that covered the window. The man stood poised at the top of the hill, near the barn. He turned his ear, listening.

As she watched, he reached for the barn door.

Tears burned Rosie's eyes. In another second, he would find them.

"May I help you?"

Hearing Ezra's voice, Rosie shifted her gaze to where he stood near Katherine's house.

"You're the guy in the buggy," Wagner shouted back. "I thought you didn't know where Katherine Runnals lived."

Ezra ignored the comment. "What do you want?"

"I'm looking for a young Amish woman with blond hair. She worked at Shady Manor, the nursing home in town. She needs to pick up her paycheck."

"You work there?" Ezra asked.

"I know the manager and told him I would help locate his missing employee."

"Buses leave from town every day. Your missing Amish woman is probably on her way to another state. Florida is a favorite destination for many Amish in the area."

Wagner sniffed and shook his head with frustration. He glanced back at the barn and pulled in a deep breath before heading back to his car.

Rosie's knees went weak. She let out the breath she had been holding and cuddled Joseph closer to her heart.

"Thank You, *Gott*," she said. "Thank You for providing this barn in which to hide, and thank You for sending Ezra to distract Mr. Wagner just a second before he would have found us."

Once again, Ezra had come to their rescue.

As soon as the SUV turned out of the drive and headed back down the mountain, Ezra ran up the hill toward the cluster of pines. His heart stopped. The buggy was gone. So was Rosie.

Hearing a weak cry, Ezra hurried along the path, following the sound that grew stronger. The cry—a baby's cry—was coming from the dilapidated barn.

He threw open the door.

Rosie gasped with surprise.

Ezra ran to her, his heart nearly bursting with relief. "I feared Wagner would find you."

"He almost did. But *Gott* provided."

Ezra was not sure whether *Gott* had intervened, but he was overcome with gratitude that Rosie and Joseph were safe.

"What about my aunt?"

"No one answered the door so she must not be home." Ezra motioned Rosie toward the door. "We must leave the barn and go farther up the mountain. You will be safe at my house."

"Are you sure?" Her eyes were filled with questions.

"You can trust me," he said, hoping she believed him. After everything that had happened, he wondered if she trusted anyone.

"Perhaps we need to involve law enforcement, Rosie. The police in this area are not helpful. Some say they have their hand out and their eyes closed. It is different in Willkommen, some miles from here. The town has a sheriff who understands the Amish way. He was injured some time ago and is still recuperating, but an acting sheriff is filling his spot, and is well-thought-of by *Englisch* and Amish alike. We can talk to him if need be."

Rosie shook her head. "Not now. I do not want to involve anyone else at this time. Mr. Wagner will eventually give up his search for me, Ezra. If I can stay with you and your brothers and sisters for a short time, that will be a help. I must contact Katherine's daughter about a place to stay in Ohio. Perhaps she will take me in until I can find a job there."

"Ohio is a long way from Georgia."

Rosie nodded. "This is true, which means a long way from Larry Wagner."

And a long way from Ezra. He did not want to think about Rosie leaving the mountain. To go so far away would end any hope Ezra had of getting to know her better. Pretty and courageous, Rosie would find an Amish man in Ohio who would take interest in her. She would forget about all she left behind, including Ezra.

After the adrenaline rush of nearly being confronted by Larry Wagner, Rosie now sat in the buggy next to Ezra, feeling totally depleted. She also felt a bone-chilling cold that was due to the drop in temperature, and also to the realization of how twisted her life had become.

Joseph was awake but content and warm in her arms. Tears stung her eyes when she thought of what could have happened to her child.

"Ezra, you have done so much for me, but I have something to ask of you."

He must have heard the seriousness in her voice because he pulled up on the reins and stopped the buggy. Turning to her, he nodded as if encouraging her to continue.

"If—if something happens to me—"

"What are you talking about, Rosie?" His face was washed with a mix of worry and concern.

She raised her hand to stop him so she could explain what she needed.

"I am worried about Joseph. If something happens to me, will you ensure he is reunited with either my mother or Katherine?"

"Rosie, you and Joseph will both be safe at my house. Wagner thinks you have left the area. You do not need to worry."

"I fear you are too optimistic, Ezra. As much as I appreciate your help, and I do so much, I still must know that my son will not be abandoned. He is all I have, and I am all he has. To find peace, I must know he will be cared for."

Ezra nodded. He reached for her hand. His eyes were as blue as the nearby lake, flecked with gold and filled with tenderness that was like a balm to her troubled soul.

"Joseph will be well cared for, this I promise. We have a full house at the mountaintop, but we always have room for more. If your mother or aunt are not able to care for him, he will come into my family. You will see how quickly my brothers and sisters accept him."

He pointed ahead. "The house is not far. Shake off your concerns. My family will welcome you, Rosie. They will welcome little Joseph, too."

True to his word, Ezra guided the buggy around the bend in the path, where she caught sight of a rambling house that sat almost at the top of the mountain. An expansive yard surrounded the home and a drive led from the road to the wide back porch. A tin roof stretched over the rear of the house and the door that, she surmised, led to the kitchen.

"The two younger children are at school, but Susan, Aaron and Belinda should be at home." He pulled the horse to a stop, climbed from the buggy and hurried to the far side to help Rosie down.

Carrying Joseph in her arms, she glanced back at the panoramic view of the valley that spread out in front of the house. "It is so peaceful. The view reminds me of a painting of the Alps that hangs in Shady Manor."

"I have heard many things about these mountains, but never has anyone compared them to the Alps."

"The beauty, Ezra. It takes my breath way."

"Which is not good. I want you to keep breathing."

She laughed, seeing the seriousness he tried to exude while the joviality of his voice gave away his true feelings.

She glanced at the far side of the property to where a workshop stood. Stoltz Buggy Shop, the sign over the door read.

"Your father was well-known for his craftsmanship. I have heard my father mention his work. I am sorry about what happened."

Ezra nodded, his frivolity gone, replaced with a tightness that revealed the pain he still carried. His parents had been murdered sixteen months earlier, if Rose recalled clearly. Not long before Will was killed. Life had changed for both Rose and Ezra at that time. Darkness had overshadowed each of their lives. She still felt that darkness no matter how much she wanted to move into the light.

She glanced again at the road that twisted up the mountain. No matter what Ezra said, she was vulnerable even here.

"What will stop the man from finding me, Ezra?"

He pointed to the roadway that snaked up the mountain. "We will see his car, Rosie. He will not approach us without warning."

"And if he comes at night when we are sleeping?"

"Then I will ward him off and keep him away from you. You have my promise."

The door to the kitchen burst open and a pretty girl in her late teens stepped onto the porch. "You have brought company," she said, stretching out her hand to grip Rosie's. "Welcome. I am Susan, the oldest girl in the family."

"This is Rose Glick and her son, Joseph. They will be staying with us for a period of time."

A hint of confusion washed over the younger woman's face before she pointed to the kitchen. "It is cold. Let us enter the house. I have hot coffee and cinnamon rolls that have just come from the oven. You are hungry?"

Rosie had thought only of Joseph's hunger and not her own, but the mention of fresh-baked rolls made her realize how hungry she was.

"Both sound inviting, Susan. You are as generous as your brother."

She followed Susan into the house and was taken with the well-appointed kitchen, the quality of the oak table, sideboard and dry sink, as well as the furnishings in the main room, visible from where she stood near the door.

"Come in. The heat from the stove will warm you along with the coffee."

"Could I wash my hands first?"

"Of course." Susan stretched out her arms. "Let me hold your son while you remove your cape. You will find a basin and pitcher of water in the small room to the right."

"You've been so kind." As much as Rosie did not want

to leave Joseph, she saw the eagerness and excitement in Susan's blue eyes as she held out her hands. Joseph loved people and had never been shy around strangers, so Rosie felt sure he would go to Susan readily. And that was the case. "I shall be back momentarily."

Rosie washed and dried her hands and returned soon thereafter to retrieve her little one. She found Joseph sitting in a high chair that looked handcrafted. Seeing her as she entered the kitchen, he kicked his legs and his hands waved in the air. He laughed and his merriment filled the kitchen and brought a smile not only to her face, but also to her heart.

"You have a big boy chair," Rosie said to her son. She glanced at Susan. "The craftsmanship is lovely."

"Our father made the high chair for Ezra, but all of us used it. We keep it in the pantry for when friends visit with small children."

"Thank you for letting Joseph sit in such a special chair. You are both very thoughtful."

"I gave him a tiny morsel of roll," Susan admitted. "I hope you do not mind."

Rosie smiled at the powdered sugar icing that ringed his lips. She stepped closer and bent down to smile into his face. "You love Susan's rolls, I can tell." Taking a napkin from the table, she wiped his mouth. "Susan knows what you want before you even know yourself."

"She has a gift for hospitality," Ezra said. His love for his sister was evident, and that fact only made Rosie like him even more.

"I will pour coffee." Susan started to rise.

"Let me." Rosie headed to the stove and lifted the coffeepot from the rear burner. She filled one of the cups on the counter. "Coffee, Ezra?"

"Please, but you did not come here to work."

Rosie laughed. "Pouring coffee is hardly work, but work is good. I do not like to have idle hands."

"You sound like our mother," Susan reflected. "She did not want to rest until night came and it was time to sleep. She had more energy than all the rest of us together."

Rosie smiled at the shared memory. "I am sure you have inherited her appreciation for work. Your home is spotless. With such a large family, this is sometimes hard to do."

"We all work together," Susan said sweetly.

"Your parents would be proud of you." Rosie looked at Ezra. "It is hard to step into the parental role."

"No one can take their place," Susan said. Her focus was on Joseph, and she failed to see the look of knowing that passed between Ezra and Rosie.

"Ezra is a good older brother," Susan continued. "He runs the farm well. Aaron is a help. David as well, although David sometimes thinks he can do things by himself."

"He is wise beyond his years in many ways," Ezra acknowledged, "while still a boy at other times. I did not want the younger ones to lose their innocence. Life is hard. Losing parents is especially tragic, but they have handled the loss bravely." He glanced down at his coffee. "Sometimes I think they fared better than I have."

Susan patted his hand. "They feel secure with your guidance, Ezra. You have given up your freedom, the freedom you sought. This has been one of the many gifts you have given the family."

He drank deeply from his cup and then pushed back

from the table. "I must unhitch the mare and get to the chores. The day will be gone if I do not start working."

He glanced at Susan. "You will show Rosie to the guest room."

"Yes, of course." She smiled at Rosie. "You might want to rest for a bit. Joseph can stay with me."

Much as Rosie did not want to be a burden to Ezra's family, she appreciated the offer, and from Joseph's laughter, it was evident Susan had stolen his heart.

"You do not mind?" Rosie asked.

"I would not offer if it was not something that I wanted to do."

"Perhaps resting for a few minutes would be good. But if Joseph becomes unsettled or too much for you, let me know."

"The guest room is at the top of the stairs to the left. The linens on the bed are fresh."

Rosie sipped the rest of her coffee and carried the cup to the sink. Looking out the window, she could see the road below. If what Ezra said was true, the family would know if anyone approached the mountaintop from the road. Larry Wagner would not surprise them. Tonight she would worry more about her safety, but now, in the light of day, she felt secure.

She turned and found Ezra staring at her. His gaze burned into her as if he wanted to tell her something more.

Her heart lurched in response, causing a wave of concern to wash over her. She might be secure from Larry Wagner today, but Ezra was another problem. The way she responded to his closeness and his concern for her well-being brought another fear to her heart. How could she leave the mountain and Ezra and head north, knowing she would never see his welcoming smile or understanding eyes again?

She had noticed him in school years earlier, although she had not, at the time, understood her own attraction to the handsome boy three years her senior. Now she realized the truth of those feelings. Ezra was a *gut* man. He would make some woman a fine husband, but that woman was not Rosie. She had to put Joseph's needs first, which meant leaving the mountain and everyone she knew to start a new life. A life without Ezra.

TEN

Ezra tackled the chores with a vengeance, as if wanting to fight off the feelings for Rosie that were taking hold inside him. He also wanted to crush Larry Wagner, who had caused her so much pain. He cleaned the stalls and the tack, rubbing the saddles with soap and wiping them clean until they glistened in the light from the window.

A fence needed mending on the distant pasture, but he did not want to stay away from the house for a long time, lest something happen while he was gone. He remembered too well the terrible tragedy that had befallen his parents.

A robbery gone wrong, the police had proclaimed.

Very wrong... Ezra's stomach tightened. Their murder had been due to his own desire to live life to the fullest. Only he had brought pain and grief to himself and his family.

Foolish and stupid. He felt as slimy as the muck he raked from the stalls.

Worried that the cattle would find the hole in the fencing, he saddled one of the geldings and rode to the distant pasture. Working quickly, he fixed the fence temporarily to keep the animals contained.

As he galloped back to the house, his heart nearly stopped when he saw a car heading up the hill. White, but not a SUV. He breathed out the deep breath he had been holding, slipped from the saddle and guided the horse into the barn minutes before the car pulled to a stop.

A man dressed in a blue uniform stepped from the unmarked vehicle. He was in his early forties with a thick neck and deep-set eyes. He nodded to Ezra.

"I'm Officer Vincetti, and I'm trying to find a woman who worked in town at the Shady Manor nursing home. She's Amish with blond hair and blue eyes. Her name is Rosie Glick."

"This is the Stoltz farm. Perhaps you could check in town for the address of the Glick family."

The officer nodded. "I am aware of who you are, but I hoped you would have information about Ms. Glick."

"She has done something wrong?"

"That's what I need to find out."

Ezra said nothing and hoped his silence might encourage the officer to provide more information. Thankfully his plan brought success.

"Ms. Glick has been accused of breaking into a secured area of patient records," the officer volunteered. "Some drugs have also gone missing, which is why I need to talk to her."

"Has she been accused of taking the medication?"

"The manager of the nursing home has mentioned her possible involvement."

"And this man is to be trusted or is he overlooking his own mishandling of medication?" Ezra asked.

The cop raised an eyebrow. "The manager is well-thought-of in town, Mr. Stoltz. Is there something you would like to share with me?"

"Only that the Amish make easy targets. We keep to ourselves, and our ways are sometimes hard for the *Englisch* to understand. Integrity is the hallmark of an Amish man or woman. I wonder if you are looking in the wrong community for the thief."

"Do you know anything about Rosie Glick?" the officer persisted.

"I know that if she is Amish, she can be trusted."

"If you see Rosie Glick, let me know." The officer handed him a business card.

"I do not have a phone on which to call you."

Vincetti nodded. "I know many of the Amish have cell phones or telephone booths near their property. You should be able to contact me."

"I appreciate your attempt to rid the town of crime, but this time of year, many Amish visit family or go on vacations. Pinecraft, Florida, is a well-known destination. Perhaps you should search there."

The officer glanced at the house and honed in on the guest-room window, which made Ezra uneasy. Hopefully, Rosie was asleep and not peering from the window.

The door to the kitchen opened. Ezra swallowed hard. He wanted to warn Rosie to stay inside, but instead of Rosie, Susan appeared.

"Is something wrong, Ezra?" she asked.

"Nothing, Susan. It is cold out here. Go into the house."

The policeman watched her go back inside. Then he rubbed his chin. "As I recall, you ran with a bunch of bad boys in town. People say you changed after your parents died, but I'm not so sure. If there's something you're not telling me, I'll find out. Do you understand?"

Ezra continued to stare at Vincetti until he climbed into his sedan and drove back down the hill.

Ezra let out a deep sigh of relief and glanced at the guest-room window, where Rosie stood staring down at him, her gaze filled with questions.

Ezra had told her she did not need to worry, but he was wrong. A case of tampering with records and stealing drugs was being made against her. A very strong case.

What have I done bringing her here?

He turned and walked into the barn, trying to sort through the mystery that was Rosie Glick. Surely, she was not guilty of criminal activity. But one thing was certain—Rosie Glick was keeping secrets.

Rosie's stomach churned. She rubbed her hand across her midsection, hoping to quell her upset. She had awakened to the sound of an automobile pulling into the drive. Fearing it was a white SUV driven by the man who kept coming after her, she had thrown back the quilt, climbed from the bed and hurried to the window.

Relieved not to see an SUV, she soon realized the visitor was anything but friendly, yet Ezra seemed to chat with him as if they were buddies. Were they? If so, had he told the policeman about the woman hiding out in his guest room? A woman suspected of tampering with patient records and stealing patient medication? Drugs that could be sold on the street?

She raked her hand through her hair, unfazed when her bun came loose and her hair fell askew over her shoulders. How foolish of her to place her trust in Ezra. The boy she remembered had a sharp edge at times, in spite of the help he gave the teacher with the stove and other chores. He never seemed totally happy and would often stare out the window as if willing himself to be anywhere but school.

Like Rosie, he had run with a bunch of *Englisch-ers*. She understood that wanderlust that made everything outside the Amish way look inviting. How quickly she had succumbed to its lure. But she had even more quickly realized her mistake.

Now she embraced the Amish way and wanted nothing to do with anything of the world. She was not sure where Ezra stood. He had come home to care for his siblings, and that was admirable. But where was his heart? Was it still on the other side of the divide between the *plain* life and that which was *fancy*?

Plus, she feared he had contacted the police, although she did not know how. Did he have a cell phone?

Her hands trembled as she tried to redo her hair, bemoaning the strands that refused to comply. They were as she had been in her younger years, rebellious and hard to handle. No wonder her father had not welcomed her back into their home. Although even if Joseph did something to upset her, she could never turn her back on her own child.

She hurried all the more to tidy her hair, before she slipped the *kapp* over her bun and scurried out of the room, needing to see her baby and hold him in her arms. Joseph was the only one she trusted. He gave meaning to her life. She would do anything for her child, yet she had left him with a stranger, nice though Susan was. Tears burned Rosie's eyes. How weak she had been, choosing sleep over the security of her little one.

Rosie ran down the stairs, nearly tripping over her feet, which would not move fast enough. Breathless, she bounded into the kitchen, almost ready to cry.

Ezra pushed open the door and stepped inside, bringing with him the clean, sweet-smelling fresh air of the outdoors. His gaze caught hers, questions filling his eyes, but she saw something else that tangled around her spine and made her stop short. Not fear, not worry, but attraction that was raw and uninvited. His look made her heart lurch and her chest tighten and a delicious warmth spread over her.

"You are in a hurry?" he asked.

She glanced around the kitchen. "Where is Joseph?"

"In here, Rosie." Susan's voice sounded from the living area.

Rosie rounded the corner and laughed when she saw Joseph standing up, holding onto Susan's hands and taking feeble steps forward. His giggles made her fear flee. Still awash with the warmth from Ezra's glance, Rosie felt weak yet also confused about being in this strange man's house.

"Joseph is walking," Susan said with joy. "He is so proud of his accomplishments."

Unable to contain her relief, Rosie clapped her hands and reached for her baby boy, drawing him close before she twirled him around the room. "You are so adventurous, trying to walk with Susan. I was worried *Mamm* had slept too long. In fact if I had slept longer you would probably be running around the downstairs without me being able to catch you."

Joseph giggled and wrapped his arms though her unkempt hair. Then he placed his wet mouth against her cheek in the sweetest kiss she had ever received.

Laughing with contentment, she stopped to enjoy the moment and then glanced up to see Ezra staring at both of them. The pain on his face confused her. Was he jealous of her son or upset that she was having fun with her baby?

She hugged Joseph closer, unwilling to let her moment of happiness be spoiled by a man she did not understand.

She and Joseph would leave the mountain as soon as possible. First, she must talk to Katherine and find information about Alice. Then she and Joseph would take the next bus to Ohio. They would make their new home there, far from the man in the SUV and far from Ezra and the confusion he made her feel.

Ezra stomped across the kitchen, ready to go outside again and head for the pasture. He had been foolish to think Rosie needed twenty-four-hour protection. A policeman had come to the house, but he had not found her. Hopefully, Ezra's hinting that she was headed to Florida would make them look south and not at the top of the mountain.

When he reached for the kitchen door, it flew open and David and Mary hurried inside with books in their arms. Both of them had rosy cheeks and windblown hair.

"Ezra," they both squealed, throwing themselves into his arms. Their warm welcome pushed away the sorrow he had felt seeing Rosie embrace her little Joseph. Sorrow had welled up within him thinking of his own parents, who had encircled him with their arms when he was young. The parents who had been murdered because of him so that none of the children would know the care and concern that came from a loving *mamm* and *datt*.

He dropped to his knees and drew his siblings closer.

"We both did well on our math tests," David boasted. "Mary made one mistake, and I made none."

"You are star students." Ezra felt a swell of pride, as if he was their father.

"Teacher says we must be working hard at home to learn our lessons so well," Mary said, her eyes wide.

"Your teacher is right," Ezra agreed, knowing both children took their studies seriously.

"Can Miss Gingrich come for dinner sometime, Ezra? She is very pretty." His little sister's eyes widened, and she nodded as she spoke as if to underscore the validity of what she said.

"Miss Gingrich is a pretty lady," Ezra replied, "but we will wait for a bit before we invite her."

"Why?"

He smiled at Mary's upset. "Because we have visitors."

"Where are they?" She pushed past him and stopped at the threshold to the main room. No doubt, she had expected a familiar face and was taken aback seeing Rosie and Joseph.

"My name is Mary." She introduced herself to Rosie. "I am seven years old."

"It is nice to meet you. I am Rosie and this is Joseph. He is eight months old. Your sister Susan has been teaching him to walk."

Mary stepped closer. "Will you let him walk so I can see?"

Joseph cooed at Mary and reached for her as if an instant connection had been made between them. As Ezra watched, Rosie placed Joseph on the floor and then encouraged him to stand while she held his hands. He took two steps forward, giggled at Mary and then dropped to the floor and crawled toward her.

"Looks like he prefers his old mode of transportation," Rosie laughed.

Mary sat on the floor and held out her arms. Joseph crawled into her lap, looking proud of himself as he smiled first at Rosie and then at Mary.

"He likes me." The little girl laughed.

"He does," Rosie agreed.

David was more unassuming than his sister. He glanced at Ezra as if for support and then turned his gaze to Rosie.

She motioned him forward. "You must have a name."

"His name is David," Mary volunteered.

"Joseph would like to play with you, too, David," Rosie declared.

The boy ran to the corner and grabbed a few wooden blocks. "We can build a tower." He dumped the scraps of wood on the floor and started to stack them. Joseph grabbed a piece and waved it in the air before he dropped it on top of the other blocks.

As the children laughed, Rosie joined Ezra in the kitchen. "You have a lovely family," she told him.

"You have yet to meet Aaron and Belinda," he said. "They will be home soon."

"I am sure they are as enchanting as the others."

"*Enchanting* is not how I think of my family."

"Perhaps because you are so close to them and do not see the specialness of each of them. You are a fortunate man, Ezra."

Although he knew that to be true, at times he would not accept the goodness that surrounded him and made him feel even worse for the pain he had caused his family.

"I appreciate your comment, Rosie."

She rubbed her arm as if feeling ill at ease. Glancing

again at the children, she smiled before turning back to him. "I saw you talking to the police officer. Did you call him?"

Ezra heard accusation in her voice. "Why would I do that?" he asked.

"To find out more about me perhaps?"

"I know all I need to know about you, Rosie, and I believe everything you have told me. The policeman stopped here on his own."

"Was he looking for me?"

Ezra could not hide the truth from her. "He was looking for you, *yah*."

"What did you tell him?"

"That you were probably on a bus heading south."

"Did he believe you?"

"I do not know. The manager of the nursing home told him you broke into patient records and that medication was stolen."

"He will arrest me if he finds me."

"The police want to question you, but as I told you before, the Amish do not trust the local police. If we go to Willkommen—"

She shook her head. "I want nothing to do with the police."

"I am not sure how long it will be before someone sees you, Rosie."

She bit her lip. "Earlier you assured me of my safety if I came here to stay with your family. Now you realize I am placing all of you in danger."

"I did not say that. I am worried about you. Would it not be better to involve law enforcement we could trust?"

She nodded. "If we could trust them. I am not willing

to put my life and my child's life in the hands of someone I do not know."

"The police took you home after you were freed from the root cellar."

"You know the story?"

"Only the part I read in the papers."

"My memory is not always good," she admitted. "So much happened. Yes, an officer took me home, but my father was not happy about my homecoming or what the officer said to him. I do not want any involvement with them again. If this is something you cannot condone, Ezra, then I am ready to go elsewhere."

He almost laughed at her sincerity, knowing she had nowhere to go except her aunt's house, where she would be even more vulnerable.

"You can stay here, Rosie, for as long as you need to. As I said earlier, I will do everything I can to keep you safe. I did not call the police, nor will I involve any law enforcement unless you request that I do so."

He grabbed his hat from the peg by the door. "You may question my integrity, but I will not cause you pain, at least if I can help it. I have made mistakes, *yah*. But I feel you know about mistakes, Rosie, and carry a similar pain. Nothing will make me disparage you or undermine your trust."

ELEVEN

The smells of bacon, sizzling in a skillet, and fresh-baked biscuits hot from the oven woke Rosie with a start the next morning.

She rubbed her eyes and pulled herself from bed, realizing she had slept more soundly than she had in months.

Peering into the portable crib Sandra had found in the basement, Rosie smiled, seeing Joseph's sweet face. His mouth opened and closed as if searching for food. He would wake soon, ready for breakfast.

She dressed and got Joseph ready for the new day before heading downstairs. Susan greeted her with a big smile before her attention turned to Joseph. "How is that big boy who wants to walk?"

He giggled in reply and kicked his feet.

"Let me get him settled in the high chair, Susan. He needs to eat to get energy for his walking exercise today."

"You are too precious," Susan said, bending over him, making him laugh even more. "There is a sippy cup in the cabinet, if you want him to use it. I have a pot of oatmeal on the stove."

Rosie appreciated the offers. "He would love oatmeal.

I will cut up a portion of a biscuit into little bites and fill the sippy cup with water."

"Bananas are in the pantry, if he likes fruit."

"What does he not like?" Rosie laughed.

"He is a big boy. Does he take after his father?"

Rosie hesitated, then shook off her uneasiness. "He looks like both sides of the family. Speaking of family, where are the children?"

"Tending to their chores. They will come inside soon."

"Shall I pour milk for David and Mary?"

"Please, I appreciate the help. Belinda is checking the henhouse for more eggs. She should be here soon."

"I enjoyed talking with her and Aaron over dinner last night. They both seem to know what they want for the future and are committed to staying in town and staying Amish."

"That is due to Ezra. He has worked hard to make sure they understand everything that is good about the Amish way."

"It is what Ezra believes?" Rosie asked.

Susan glanced at her for a long moment. "I am not sure for himself, but for them, it is the best path."

"I know he got involved with the *Englisch*."

Susan nodded. "In his *rumspringa*, only it lasted longer than anyone expected. He stayed away from home and rarely returned to see *Mamm* and *Datt*. They did not expect such actions from their firstborn son, but Ezra needed to do what was right for himself."

"And now?"

"You will have to ask him."

Something Rosie would not do. "Will you be at home today?"

Susan nodded. "*Yah*. There is something you need?"

"I need to talk to a nurse with whom I worked. But I do not want to take Joseph. I need someone to watch him. Would you be interested?"

"Of course, I would love to take care of him. He is so sweet. He has his mother's disposition."

Rosie smiled, appreciating Susan's statement.

"Will you ring the dinner bell?" Susan asked. "It will call the family. I do not want the breakfast to get cold."

Rosie stepped onto the porch and found the metal gong hanging near the large, steel triangle. She hit the gong against the triangle, enjoying the mellow sound of metal on metal. For a fleeting moment, she thought of calling her own family to breakfast.

Ezra hurried from the barn and stopped when he saw her. His face broke into a wide grin. "I feared something was wrong."

"Nothing is wrong except your breakfast is getting cold."

"I will gather the children."

She liked the sound of the comment, thinking of her own children hurrying inside after doing the chores with their father.

But when she stepped inside, Joseph was crying. The sound tore into her heart.

"Something is wrong?" She glanced at Susan.

"He took a drink from the cup and started to cry. I wonder if he hurt himself."

Rosie lifted his upper lip and felt his gums. She nodded knowingly. "His gums are swollen and red. I believe he is getting a tooth. He may have clamped down on the sippy cup and hurt his gums.

"Shh," she soothed.

His crying waned when Mary stepped into the

kitchen. In an instant, he was kicking his feet in happiness, tears forgotten.

Rosie wiped his nose with a tissue and then washed her hands before the rest of the children raced inside, bringing in the cool morning air and the freshness of a new day.

Ezra was the last to enter, his eyes twinkling, his cheeks ruddy. Rosie was hard-pressed to keep her eyes averted, and she caught herself turning to stare at him. He patted Joseph's head, making the baby laugh all the more, and then held a chair away from the table for Rosie.

She did not know what to say and so she said nothing.

David chuckled.

Ezra gave him a stern glare. "Young man, you can help your sister with her chair."

"What?" David looked aghast.

"First Belinda and then Mary."

The boy rolled his eyes but dutifully held his older sister's chair.

"Thank you, David," Belinda said, her smile proof she appreciated the gesture.

Mary pulled out her own chair. "I can seat myself all by myself."

Ezra laughed. "Someday, Miss Mary, you will enjoy a man's help."

"I would let Joseph help me with my chair," she said, waving to the baby, who waved back, his hand slapping the air with enthusiasm.

"Why were you crying?" she asked him.

"Joseph is getting a tooth," Rosie explained. "His gums hurt when he bit down on the cup as he tried to take a drink of water."

Mary pointed to the cup. "Take small sips, Joseph, and be careful not to spill your water or hurt your mouth."

"You are a good teacher, Mary." Rosie appreciated the children, who made her feel so welcome and seemed to enjoy having Joseph with them. In her parents' house, she had felt like a stranger who was not welcome. Here was just the opposite.

Ezra glanced at her and smiled. Silly of her to have gotten upset with him yesterday. He was a *gut* man and a loving brother who was putting his family before his own needs.

After Mary and David left for school, Rosie helped Susan with the dishes while Ezra worked on a broken fence. He had cautioned the women to keep watch on the roadway and to ring the dinner bell if they saw a car approaching.

Today, the fear Rosie had felt seemed distant. She had slept well and laughed with the children and everything that had happened seemed as if it was at another time or had happened to another person.

Then she thought of Mr. Calhoun, who had died, and the missing medication.

Ezra returned to the house and smiled as he entered the kitchen, filling her with gratitude for his help. "I know you have much work to do," she said, "but I wondered if we could talk to Nan today about her visit to the pharmacist and what she learned about Mr. Calhoun's death."

"You and I are thinking similar thoughts. Although I do not want you on the road until more time has passed. I will go alone."

"Susan said she can watch Joseph, and I would like

to go with you, although I agree about the main roads. What about the back trails we were on yesterday?"

"This would work although some are narrow that weave toward town, especially around the mountain area where Nan lives."

"Can you ride?" Susan asked. "Belinda and I ride our horses to town sometimes. The riding paths are shorter than the paved roads, and if we do not have a lot of groceries to carry, we can do our errands and get home in a much shorter time."

Rosie looked down at her dress. "I ride, but this is all I have to wear."

Susan laughed. "Which is not a problem. My sister and I wear pants under our skirts. You are more slender than I am, but we can pin the waist. Today is warmer than yesterday. I have a wool sweater you can wear under your cape."

"Then it is decided," Rosie said with a nod. "We will ride to Nan's house and find out what she learned about Mr. Calhoun's death and the missing medication."

Ezra saddled the horses—Duke and Duchess—and brought them to the back of the house. Rosie hugged Joseph and thanked Susan again for staying with her baby.

Wearing the pants under her skirt and the heavy sweater along with her cape, Rosie was comfortable. "I used to ride when I was a girl," she told Ezra as he held the stirrup and helped her into the saddle. She took the reins. "This is like going back in time."

"To a good place, I hope," he said.

She nodded. "Yes, a good time and place. When I was young, my father was a caring man who I knew loved me. He changed over time."

"Perhaps he did not want his daughter to grow up.

Can you pinpoint something that happened when he started to change?"

She shook her head. "The only thing I remember is that we went to town when I was thirteen. A man standing on the street corner said I was a pretty girl and asked my father if he could take my photograph."

"I do not think this would be something your father would want for his young daughter."

"He did not answer the man, but he grabbed my hand and jerked me into the nearest store. Then he kept watch at the store window until the man left the street and drove away. From that time on, my father acted as if I had done something wrong, as if I had encouraged the man in some way."

"You are beautiful, Rosie. Your father must have realized his little girl was growing up."

She shook her head, not willing to accept his statement. She was not beautiful. She was headstrong and self-centered, and she had brought too much pain to her family. She did not deserve their love or attention, and her father was probably correct in realizing what would happen, as if the man's attention had been a prophetic warning about her wayward future.

She grabbed the reins from Ezra and held the horse back until he had climbed on Duke, then she encouraged Duchess forward and headed for the front gate.

"Rosie, wait. You and Duchess are going in the wrong direction."

She pulled up on the reins and glanced over her shoulder at Ezra. He pointed to a trail near the one that had brought them to the house yesterday.

"We will ride this way unless you have changed your mind about wanting to take the back trails."

She had almost left Ezra. She was too focused on herself instead of others, just as her father had told her on more than one occasion.

"I will follow your lead," she said, feeling a bit ashamed of her impetuousness. Amish women were to be subdued and subordinate. Would she never learn her place in the Amish world?

"FAST FIVE" READER SURVEY

Your participation entitles you to:
✳ 4 Thank-You Gifts Worth Over $20!

Complete the survey in minutes.

Get **2 FREE** Books

See inside for details.

Dear Reader,

Since you are a lover of our books, your opinions are important to us... and so is your time.

That's why we made sure your **"FAST FIVE" READER SURVEY** can be completed in just a few minutes. Your answers to the five questions will help us remain at the forefront of women's fiction.

And, as a thank-you for participating, we'd like to send you **4 FREE THANK-YOU GIFTS!**

Enjoy your gifts with our appreciation,

Pam Powers

To get your
4 FREE THANK-YOU GIFTS:

✳ Quickly complete the "Fast Five" Reader Survey
and return the insert.

"FAST FIVE" READER SURVEY

1 Do you sometimes read a book a second or third time? ○ Yes ○ No

2 Do you often choose reading over other forms of entertainment such as television? ○ Yes ○ No

3 When you were a child, did someone regularly read aloud to you? ○ Yes ○ No

4 Do you sometimes take a book with you when you travel outside the home? ○ Yes ○ No

5 In addition to books, do you regularly read newspapers and magazines? ○ Yes ○ No

YES! I have completed the above Reader Survey. Please send me my 4 FREE GIFTS (gifts worth over $20 retail). I understand that I am under no obligation to buy anything, as explained on the back of this card.

❏ I prefer the regular-print edition
153/353 IDL GM3W

❏ I prefer the larger-print edition
107/307 IDL GM3W

FIRST NAME	LAST NAME

ADDRESS

APT.#	CITY

STATE/PROV.	ZIP/POSTAL CODE

TWELVE

Ezra was impressed with Rosie's riding ability and enjoyed the sunshine and crisp morning air. The temperature seemed mild after the recent cold spell. Rosie's cheeks were pink with exertion, and her laughter floated across the fields, filling him with happiness. If only life could be this freeing. Both Ezra and Rosie needed time away from the worries and cares that had surrounded them since he had followed her out of town just a few days ago.

At the top of a rise, he pulled up on the reins and waited for Rosie to join him.

"It's beautiful here," she said as her horse sidled next to his. "I had forgotten how much I enjoy riding. It takes me back to my youth. To a better time."

He understood. "As a boy, I rode all over the mountain. Often my mother would send me on an errand to town, but other times when my chores were done, I would come up here to dream of what my future would be."

"You dreamed of what, Ezra?"

He shrugged. "Adventure. Travel. Being famous. Foolish dreams, my father told me when I tried to share my thoughts with him."

"And your mother?"

"She would listen and smile without finding fault." He smiled at Rosie. "Mothers are like that, *yah*. They allow their children to dream."

"Did she worry about you leaving the faith?"

"She said I would find my way." He stared into the horizon, thinking of the painful journey he had traveled in order to find the way his mother had mentioned. Even now, he was not sure what the future would hold or where he would be years from now.

"My father always admonished me to never stray from being Amish," Rosie said. "Yet too often, he stayed away from church and refused to visit relatives and friends on the other Sundays."

"Was he a recluse or just shy?"

"Perhaps an unhappy man who never fit in."

"You left home because of him."

She jerked her head to stare at Ezra. "What did you say?"

"He is the reason you fell in love with Will MacIntosh."

"I fell in love with William because I was foolish, naive and wanted much more than the Amish way would provide. I wanted worldly happiness."

"You wanted love, the love your father should have given you, Rosie. When you did not find it within the family, you looked for it elsewhere."

She sighed. "You are passing the responsibility of my actions onto my father. They were my sins."

"Think what you like, Rosie Glick, but the need to be loved is man's most important need. Everything hinges around whether we feel loved and lovable. The love we long for most deeply within our hearts, within our beings, is our love for *Gott*. Yet He is not visible to us so we must find earthly love that teaches us what true love, the love that comes from *Gott*, is about. The father is the most important person in a girl's life as far as her feelings of acceptance and self-worth. If a father shirks his responsibility and does not adequately love his daughter, she will always search for that love, but as I mentioned, in the wrong places or with the wrong people."

"You sound like a philosopher. How did you get so knowledgeable?"

"I went to the library after my parents were murdered. I needed to decide how I could best help my siblings heal. I read over and over about a father's love. I had taken my father from his daughters so I had a responsibility to bridge that gap and fill in the void I had created."

"You talk as if you were responsible for your parents' deaths."

"I was." With a slap of the reins against his horse's rump, Ezra rode off, leaving Rosie to stare after him.

He had said too much just as he was wont to do around her. He had never told anyone about the guilt he carried. He did not need to share his own pain, but somehow Rosie made him want to bare his soul and let her see the core of who he was—a man who had caused such pain. No one would ever be able to love him when they learned the truth. A self-fulfilling prophecy, the psychology books had said.

He was getting close to Rosie, too close. He needed to let her know who he really was lest she think him something he was not. Rosie deserved a good man with an unscarred past, a man who could love her unconditionally and without hesitation. Ezra was not that man.

He looked back, watching her encourage her horse

forward. She had taken off her *kapp* and her hair had pulled free from its bun and billowed around her face and into the air as she rode. He had never seen anyone more beautiful or anyone whom he needed to avoid at all costs. He could not be attracted to Rosie or he would bring pain to her as well as to his own already broken heart.

Rosie did not understand Ezra. He shared so deeply yet when she wanted to tell him how good he really was, he rode off, not wanting praise or her words of encouragement. Perhaps he enjoyed hiding behind whatever guilt he thought he carried. Some people needed to be a victim, although Ezra did not seem like a victim. He took full responsibility for his actions and would not listen if she tried to tell him otherwise.

Ezra had not killed his parents. He had been in town, hanging out in a bar with his *Englisch* friends when his parents had been murdered. Perhaps that was his guilt. That he had not been home when he could have protected them, although he probably would have been killed as well.

He had poor hindsight, but she would not tell him that, lest he ride off again and leave her on the mountain. She needed to get to the nurse and find out what the pharmacy had said. She also hoped Nan would have news about Mr. Calhoun's death.

How could anyone think Rosie was involved in a drug racket?

Her heart skipped a beat. *William!*

Ezra had made reference to William's possible involvement, and she saw it all more clearly now. His frequent visits to a cabin in the woods, where he picked up packages wrapped like small boxes to be mailed. Only William did not go to the post office. Instead he would drive to distant towns to deliver the goods, as he called them.

Had the packages been filled with drugs?

She shivered with the realization. No wonder the nursing-home manager suspected her. Will's involvement was probably common knowledge around town or with law enforcement. She had been right not to go to the police. They would arrest her and throw her into jail.

Ezra pulled his horse to a stop and waited for Rosie.

"Nan's home is over that rise," he said. "The police want to question you, Rosie. We do not want anyone calling law enforcement about two Amish people on horseback in the area. We might be smart to weave our way through the dense wooded area and leave our horses behind the house, then we could cross Nan's backyard and arrive, hopefully unnoticed, at her house."

"That is a good plan, Ezra. I will follow you."

He guided his horse along a narrow path that led to the bottom of the incline. Rosie stayed close behind him. Once at the bottom of the hill, Ezra encouraged Duke into the wooded area.

"We are probably being overly cautious," Rosie whispered, although she appreciated Ezra's desire to keep her safe. Seeing Nan's house, she pulled up on the reins and slipped from the saddle.

"What are you doing?" Ezra asked.

"I am heading to my friend's house, knocking on the door and staying long enough to learn what she has uncovered. I do not like being a sly cat who sneaks around."

Ezra climbed down from his horse and tied the reins

to a nearby tree. He looked at her and held out his hand. "We will go together."

She slipped her hand into his, feeling the strength of his grip. They stepped into the cleared area behind Nan's house and hurried toward her back door. The bell worked but no one answered.

"Perhaps she is still at work," Rosie said.

"We are a little later than we were before," Ezra said. "She might be asleep."

Rosie rapped again on the door, and when no one answered, she pointed to the side of the house. "Nan said she can see the town lights from her bedroom window, which means it is located on that side of the house."

Together, they rounded the corner. Holding her hands around her eyes to cut down on the glare, Rosie peered through the window, grateful the blinds were partially open.

Her heart lurched. Nan lay strewn over the bed, her arms splayed, her red hair disheveled.

Rosie pounded on the window. "Nan, it is Rosie. Wake up."

Ezra stepped closer and looked through the glass.

"Something is wrong." He pulled Rosie to the back of the house. "I will ask the neighbor to call an ambulance."

Tears stung Rosie eyes. "I fear something terrible has happened. Along with the ambulance, they need to call the police."

Sirens sounded in the distance. Ezra turned to glance into the underbrush, where Rosie waited with the horses. The neighbor stood on the street to flag down the ambulance.

Ezra did not have a good feeling about what the EMTs

would find. Nan had not moved since he and Rosie had first looked through the window.

Again, he glanced at the wooded area, relieved Rosie was hidden from view. The police did not need anything additional to cause them to question her involvement in what now looked like a death investigation.

The shrill squeal of the siren neared. A police sedan turned the corner, followed by an ambulance. Both braked to a stop in front of the house.

Ezra hurried back to the wooded area where Rosie waited. Her face was pale, her mouth drawn. He squeezed her hand, hoping to provide support.

Two policemen sprang from the car. They spoke briefly to the woman on the sidewalk and then hurried to the front door. Finding it locked, they rounded to the rear, tried that door and then broke one of the side windowpanes and unlocked the door through the opening.

The police disappeared inside. Some moments later the front door opened and they beckoned to the EMTs.

Rosie stepped closer to Ezra, as if needing his reassurance. He put his arm around her shoulders. "I fear the outcome will not be good."

"They killed her, Ezra, because she was asking questions about the missing drugs. They probably killed Mr. Calhoun, too, although I do not know what he did to them. Maybe he questioned the missing medication and why he was not getting anything for his pain."

"Who are you including in the guilty?"

"The manager of the nursing home must be involved, and I saw Larry Wagner in his office the day I was fired. They fired me, thinking I was snooping around too much."

"Yet the manager let you go home."

"Mr. Wagner came to my house that night, but my parents stopped him."

"Wagner planned to apprehend you on the road, Rosie. He had damaged your bike and thought you would travel to town on foot."

"If only we knew what William was supposed to have given me."

The EMTs emerged from the house, pushing a stretcher. Nan's body was covered with a blanket.

Ezra wrapped his arm around Rosie's shoulders and felt her flinch. She turned away, no doubt, unwilling to watch her friend being placed in the ambulance.

The police questioned the neighbor and then stretched yellow police tape around Nan's house before they went to the other houses on the street gathering information.

"They are talking to the neighbors in case anyone heard or saw anything," Ezra said.

He ushered Rosie closer to Duchess. "You need to go back to my house. Wait there. I will try to find out more information."

She grabbed his hand. "You cannot stay, Ezra. They will suspect you. The neighbor has probably already told them about the Amish man who knocked on Nan's door."

"I told her that the nurse had hired me to build bookshelves for her living area. It is not unusual for Amish craftsmen to take jobs with the *Englisch*."

"But the police will take you to their headquarters for questioning."

"I will wait until the police leave. Go now, Rosie. Joseph needs you. Tell Susan I will be home later."

"Oh, Ezra—"

He placed the reins in her hand and hoisted her onto the saddle.

"I do not want to leave you," she said reluctantly before she encouraged Duchess forward through the thicket.

"Keep Rosie safe, *Gott*," Ezra murmured as he watched her find the path and head toward the mountain. She was well-protected within the forested area, and he doubted the police would notice the slight movement he saw as the horse hurried over the crest of the hill.

Turning his gaze to the street, he watched the police head back to Nan's house. One of the officers remained stationed at the front door. The other drove away in the squad car.

The neighbor with whom Ezra had spoken earlier stepped onto her back patio carrying a broom and started sweeping.

Ezra approached her, hat in hand. "Ma'am, I had to tend to my horse, but I saw you talking to the police. Do you know anything about Ms. Smith?"

"The EMTs said she overdosed. They found pills at her bedside." The woman shook her head as if unable to understand what had happened. "The pills were from the nursing home where she worked. Evidently she had been stealing drugs from the patients."

She glanced again at Ezra. "Perhaps you should talk to the police. One of them is still at the house. Do you want me to call him?"

Ezra held up his hand. "That will not be necessary. I will stop at the police station in town and talk to them there."

She nodded, as if satisfied. "It's terrible. Such a shame. You just never know about your neighbors."

The woman turned back to her house, and Ezra slipped into the woods and quickly rode up the hill.

The mountain used to be a peaceful place without crime. Once he started to associate with the *Englisch* everything changed.

He should have warned Rosie about Will MacIntosh, when he first saw them together. Had it been his pride or his upset that she was interested in another man when she had paid so little attention to him?

Perhaps he *had* been upset with her, but he should also have been upset with himself. They had both made mistakes, but neither of them were murderers or involved in a drug racket. Yet they were both being pulled into the corruption that was happening in the area.

Neither of them knew anyone who could help change this terrible situation. Not the police, not the Amish community and not the townspeople who thought the nursing-home manager was an upstanding citizen. No one would believe the Amish if they accused the good citizens of wrongdoing.

Ezra and Rosie needed to find evidence they could take to the sheriff in Willkommen to solve this tangled case involving prescription drugs. If only Will had given Rosie information, they could use that now to substantiate what they had learned.

If only, Ezra thought again.

THIRTEEN

Rosie could hardly see the path as the tears fell. She was responsible for Nan's death. The nurse had always reached out to her with kindness, yet Rosie had alerted Nan to Mr. Calhoun's pain the night he had died and had asked Nan to give him the needed pain medication. The medication, Nan all too soon realized, was missing.

Rosie tried to put the pieces together, but none of them fit. It was all so confusing. Why was she in the middle of the problem? Had Will, in some way, set her up to be a target? Did it involve whatever he was supposed to have given her? All that was wrong about their relationship was coming back to haunt her now.

If she was in danger, Joseph was as well.

She thought of Ezra's family and the innocent children. What would happen to them if the man in the white SUV stopped at their house? Would little Mary with her wide eyes and forthright nature divulge that a woman and baby were staying at their house, which would put all of them in danger? Rosie's heart ached for what could happen.

She had to leave to ensure the children were kept safe.

She would take the Amish taxi to the bus station once she learned where Katherine's daughter lived.

Money would be a problem. She had saved a little from her paychecks and had hidden it in the quilt, along with the toy Will had given her for their baby. Hopefully the cash would be enough for a bus ticket, but she would arrive in Ohio with nothing extra.

A fork in the path appeared in the distance. To the right would take her to Ezra's house. If she went left, surely it would lead to her aunt's home.

Stopping at Katherine's house would not take long. Susan had assured Rosie that she would take care of Joseph. Ezra would be at Nan's house for some time.

She tapped her heels against the horse's flank and turned him onto the other path, the one that headed, hopefully, to Katherine's house.

Rosie would be careful and watchful. She did not want another encounter with the man in the white SUV.

The trail meandered downhill. Duchess picked her way along the rocky path. Something slithered out from under a boulder. Rosie's heart lurched when she saw the snake.

The mare spooked and increased her speed. Rosie tried to hold Duchess back, but the mare refused to respond to the tug on the reins.

Duchess's trot turned to a gallop. The wind whipped at Rosie's cape and pulled at her bun.

"Oh," she groaned as the path became steeper. The horse was galloping far too fast for the treacherous terrain. Rosie should have taken the other path, the one she knew.

Once she had made sure Joseph was all right, she could have walked to Katherine's house. It would have taken more time, but at least she would not be hurling down a hillside so fast…too fast.

She pulled on the reins, hard. The mare eased up a bit and then increased her pace again.

"Oh, please," Rosie called out, not knowing what to do.

A slight rise appeared on the path ahead. The house would not be far. In the distance, Rosie saw the barn where she had hidden with the buggy yesterday and felt a swell of relief. Surely the mare would come to a stop near the structure. But the horse continued at breakneck speed. A fence appeared ahead. Instead of going around the obstacle, Duchess headed straight for it, and at the last possible moment, jumped over the barrier.

Rosie screamed. The reins slipped from her hands. She reached for the saddle horn but ended up grabbing air. The mare came down hard. Rosie slipped right. Her leg left the stirrup and without anything to hold her back, she fell.

"Oof!" Rosie landed on her side, her hand thankfully breaking her fall. Her hip ached. Dazed, she watched the mare gallop off.

So much for riding back to Ezra's house. She rubbed her head and pulled herself upright. A wave of vertigo fluttered over her. She felt her arms and legs, ensuring nothing was broken. Relieved that her limbs were intact, she tried to stand. The path swirled in front of her. She regained her balance, stepped gingerly forward with one foot and moaned. Sharp pain radiated from her ankle.

Katherine's house was not far. If she could hobble there, then perhaps she could take her aunt's buggy to Ezra's house. She felt sure he would return the buggy later in the day.

She exhaled with frustration, imagining his upset when he found out she had taken the other path, the one that led away from his house. Once again her own stubbornness had caused problems. For herself and for Ezra.

A dull ache started in her head. She rubbed her forehead, hoping to relieve the pressure that had built up there, and limped past the old, dilapidated barn to the newer one located near the house. The barn doors were open. Rosie peered inside as she passed, thinking her aunt might be working there, but the barn was empty and the buggy was gone.

Her heart plummeted. Katherine must have taken the buggy to town or she might be spending the day with friends. She could be anywhere instead of where Rosie had hoped she would be.

Standing just outside the barn, Rosie glanced down the valley, knowing she would have to walk back to Ezra's house. The trip would not be pleasant or speedy with her aching leg.

So much for her good idea. Another mistake that she could add to the list, if she was making a list. Although she would rather not put anything in writing that would show her ineptitude.

She placed her hands on her hips and sighed. A stiff wind blew her long hair into her face. Plus, she had lost her *kapp*.

Totally flummoxed and upset, she swallowed down the lump in her throat and brushed away the new rush of tears. She was becoming much too emotional.

Limping along the path, she heard a sound from the road below and turned. She blinked away the tears as her heart pounded a warning. A car was coming up the hill. A white SUV.

The man with the swatch of white hair. Larry Wagner.

Her blood chilled. She looked at the steep incline she would have to navigate to get to the path and how much farther it was to the wooded area, where she could hide.

Surely Katherine had locked her door. A few years back that was not the case and the Amish would not have secured their homes, but recently, as Rosie was all too aware, crime had come to the mountain and the Amish had started to secure their homes and their property. Except the barn was open.

Rosie headed there. She stepped inside and closed the large door behind her just as the sound of the engine announced the man had turned into the drive.

Where could she hide?

She blinked, getting used to the darkness, and headed to the stalls in the rear. Where would he first look, if he entered?

She shook her head, confused as to what to do.

Outside a car door slammed. She envisioned Wagner climbing Katherine's porch steps and heard a distant knock on the door.

A ladder led to the hayloft above. Climbing would be difficult with a twisted ankle, but she would be able to hide there out of sight. At least that was her hope.

She started up the ladder and groaned. Her leg throbbed when she put weight on it. Hiding in one of the stalls might have been a better choice.

The door to the barn started to open, sending daylight into the darkness. Ignoring the pain, she scurried up the final rungs and scooted behind the bales of hay just as Wagner stepped into the barn.

From her lofty perch, she could see him. He stepped

toward the first stall and peered inside, then went to the next one and the next.

Perhaps she had made a good decision after all to hide in the loft. Just as long as he did not look up. Fearing she might be visible, she scooted back farther, causing a bale of hay to wobble and a hen roosting there to squawk.

The hen flapped her wings and flew to the ground below.

Rosie's heart nearly leaped from her chest. She gripped her hands together as if in prayer, only words would not come. The only thing she could think of was "save me."

While *Gott* was silent, her heart was not. It pounded like a freight train.

Larry Wagner sighed. Grabbing the ladder, he climbed one rung after the other, coming closer and closer. She looked around for another exit but found none. The only thing she could do was jump down, but with her bum leg, he would surely get to her before she could escape.

Her hands were wet with sweat, her throat was dry and her pulse raged like a river down a mountain gorge. Her ears roared, yet she could hear his footfalls on each rung as he climbed.

Almost to the top, he stopped. Laughter filled the barn. His laughter.

What was so funny?

A meowing sound, followed by more laughter.

"Well, aren't you the cutest kitten ever?"

She peered from her hiding spot. A tiny kitten was perched on the edge of the loft. Wagner lifted the ball of fluff into his arms.

"What are you doing up here, scaring that ol' hen? You made me think someone was hiding from me." He laughed again. "You haven't seen a little Amish gal with blond hair, now have you, kitty? She's got something that could cause me a lot of problems if it got in the wrong hands."

The cat mewed.

"I'll come back to talk to Katherine. Maybe she'd want to give you away. I'd like a little fellow like you around." With the cat in his arms, Wagner climbed down the ladder.

Rosie rested her head against the bale of hay. The sound of his car backing out of the drive brought tears to her eyes again. She had eluded detection thanks to a small kitten. Then she realized who had protected her. She closed her eyes through the tears and gave thanks to *Gott*.

Ezra returned home and hurried into the house, expecting to find Rosie. Susan looked up from the rocking chair. Joseph was asleep in her arms.

"Where's Rosie?" his sister asked.

His heart stuttered. "She has not returned?"

"I thought she was with you."

Ezra did not wait to hear anything else Susan said. He ran to the barn, threw open the door and peered into Duchess's empty stall. Climbing back on his horse, he glanced at the trail he had just taken. The only turnoff was the path that led to Katherine's house.

Surely Rosie had not ventured there without him.

He slapped the reins and guided Duke forward along the trail Ezra and Rosie had traveled yesterday. He shook his head, mentally chastising himself. Why had he sent Rosie off alone? He could have taken the buggy to town later and made inquiries to find out what the police suspected concerning Nan's death. Instead he had allowed Rosie to travel across the countryside unprotected.

His heart ached and he wanted to scream with concern and worry and, yes, even rage, which was not the Amish way.

He had lost his parents. Would he lose another person he cared for as well?

He scanned the wooded area at the side of the paths, hoping to see some sign of her. Perhaps she had fallen off the mare and was lying at the bottom of a ravine, like when he had first found her.

Suppose the man in the SUV had her? He could have captured her and taken her—

Ezra could not think of such things or he would not be able to go on.

Katherine's house was not far ahead. Perhaps she was there, sipping tea with her aunt and sharing recipes.

If only that could be, but when he turned the bend and came out from the wooden area, he saw the barn door open and the buggy gone.

To ensure he was right, he searched the barn and knocked on the front and back doors.

"Rosie, where are you?"

The dilapidated barn sat on the rise. The old building had provided protection before. Could she have gone there again?

He stumbled over the rocks as he took a shortcut up the steep incline, needing to find her. Now. Before his heart stopped.

He pulled open the door and stepped into the dark interior, smelling the mix of hay and dung. A dove cooed from the rafters.

"Rosie?"

His heart crashed. He dropped his head into his hands. Where was she?

"Ezra?" A whisper, but her whisper, her voice, soft as silk.

"Rosie, where are you?"

"In the rear—"

Before she could finish, he was at her side, kneeling in the hay, pulling her into his arms. "Oh, Rosie, I was so worried. I thought—I thought…"

He could not say the terrible things that had run through his mind. All he could do was pull her even closer. He wove his fingers through her hair and smelled the sweet scent of her shampoo and felt the softness of her skin and the way she molded to him as if she was drowning in an ocean and he had saved her. Only he had not saved her or protected her. He had sent her away from him. Alone.

"I am so sorry and ask your forgiveness."

She did not respond, but tears fell from her eyes, wetting his shirt and making his heart break all the more.

"I am sorry," he said again, his voice little more than a whisper.

"Oh, Ezra, I am the one at fault. I took the path to Katherine's house and put myself in danger. When the man came—"

"Larry? Did he hurt you?"

She shook her head. "A kitten saved me." She smiled through her tears. "Along with help from *Gott*."

"I should have been here with you." He glanced down and saw scratches on her arms. "You are hurt."

"I fell from the horse and twisted my ankle. It will heal."

"Can you walk?"

"Not easily."

"Let me help you up." He wrapped his arms around her shoulders and guided her to her feet.

One of her legs buckled. Without effort, he lifted her into his arms. "We must hurry back to the house before Wagner returns."

Holding Rosie in his arms made Ezra's chest swell and his ears ring and his heart pound, not from fear, but from her closeness. All he wanted to do was continue to hold her. But danger was circling too close and he would not make the same mistake again.

He carried her to the door of the barn and looked outside to ensure they were alone, then he brushed his lips over her forehead, feeling like his heart would surely explode within his chest. All he had ever wanted was to hold Rosie, only not under these circumstances, not when a man who wanted to do her harm was prowling the mountain, coming closer and closer.

Ezra needed to find out the truth about what was happening at the nursing home and with the patients' drugs. Then he would make the trip to Willkommen and give the information to the sheriff or acting sheriff there. With the right evidence, they would not be able to ignore his suspicions or what he said. Ezra could not bear to have anything happen to Rosie, and right now, everyone was after her.

She was suspected of stealing drugs. For all he knew, she could also be suspected of murder, and although he had acted foolishly today, he would not let her stray from his sight until everything was out in the open and her name was cleared and the man in the SUV and the manager of the nursing home and everyone else involved in this corruption were under arrest.

FOURTEEN

Rosie did not want to put Joseph down that night. After dinner, he fell asleep in her arms. She cuddled him close as Ezra said good-night to the young children. Mary ran back to wrap her arms around Rosie's neck, and then slyly, she kissed her cheek and kissed Joseph's as well. The baby's lips twitched into a smile as if he knew sweet Mary had kissed him.

"You have been a good friend to Joseph," Rosie told the girl. "Thank you for playing with him."

"I wish he was more than a friend," Mary said as he patted his head and smiled at the sleeping child.

"More than a friend?" Rosie asked, not understanding.

The girl shrugged. "*Mamm* and *Datt* have gone to heaven so there will be no more children in our family. I do not want to be the youngest. I want a brother or sister." She looked at Rosie with big eyes. "Could Joseph be my brother?"

Rosie glanced up to see Ezra standing in the kitchen. He had, no doubt, overheard the girl's comment, but the look on his face was hard to read. Was he angry that

Mary had mentioned their parents' deaths, or was he upset that she wanted Joseph to be part of the family?

Rosie lowered her gaze, suddenly unsure of her place here. After Ezra had found her in the barn, she had never wanted to leave his arms. Undoubtedly she was dazed from everything that had happened, but she thought she had felt Ezra's lips brush against her forehead. Wishful thinking, probably, like a young schoolgirl who flirted with boys. Not that Rosie had done anything like that. She had focused on her studies, wanting to make her *datt* proud of her—something she never succeeded in doing.

Ezra had wrapped her ankle, his touch gentle, his concern sincere, which only enhanced her feelings for him. Thankfully, Duchess had returned to the barn no worse for her escapade. Rosie kept reflecting on all that had happened. Without doubt, something special had passed between them today in the barn, but now, after hearing Mary's innocent comment, Ezra seemed to stiffen and be aloof again.

She pulled Joseph closer and touched Mary's cheek with her free hand. "It is getting late. You rise early in the morning, Mary, and need your sleep. You had best go to bed."

"I will see you and Joseph tomorrow?" It was a question, as if the child was afraid they would leave, which they would do soon. But Rosie could not think of leaving sweet Mary and David, who was always so logical and tried to be grown up. Belinda, at fourteen, was blossoming into a lovely young woman ready to take on more responsibility within the family, especially if Susan had eyes on a young man in town, which is what she had surmised from some of the comments the children had made in passing.

Rosie rubbed her hand across Mary's shoulder. "Joseph will see you at breakfast." Seemingly reassured, Mary nodded and followed David upstairs.

Susan was mending a torn shirt of Aaron's, while he worked on a small propane motor that needed fixing. A knock sounded at the door. Rosie's heart raced. Ezra's face revealed the concern he felt.

Although she had not heard a car, Rosie rose and searched for a place to hide. Ezra pointed her to an alcove off the kitchen. The small area was covered by a curtain.

"Wait in there until I see who is at the door."

"Do you think—" The words would not form.

He shook his head. "I did not hear a car."

Still—

Ezra was gone, walking back through the main room toward the door. Another rap sounded.

"Who is it?" Ezra's voice was sharp and demanding.

Rosie scurried into the hiding spot, bit her lip and turned her eyes to the ceiling, trying to hear something—anything—that would give her a clue as to who had come pounding at the door.

The sound of the door opening and heavy footsteps coming to where she hid made her heart lurch.

She held her breath.

The curtain pulled back and Ezra peered in, smiling. "You can come out." His voice was low, his eyes twinkling with mirth.

"There is someone here?" she asked.

He nodded. "John Keim, from town. He is the blacksmith's son. He came to ask if Susan could accompany him to youth singing this weekend. The group will also do some caroling."

Rosie smiled. Her heart soared with joy for Susan, whose cheeks turned pink and eyes took on a softness whenever John's name was mentioned. "How does her big brother feel about someone courting his younger sister?"

"I feel like a father who does not know if he wants her daughter to grow up or stay young."

They laughed together. She glanced down at Joseph, feeling stronger. "I must put him to bed, plus it would be better if John did not see me."

"He and Susan are taking a short walk. I told them they can talk on the front porch."

"They would probably prefer the front room, although…" She smiled. "They would be alone on the porch and could huddle together to keep warm."

He laughed again, causing Joseph to startle.

"Put Joseph to bed and then come downstairs," Ezra suggested. "We can have a second cup of coffee. I do not think John will stay long."

"That sounds *gut.*"

Leaving Ezra in the kitchen waiting for her and carrying her baby upstairs felt so natural and so normal— exactly what Rosie wanted for her life. After she covered Joseph with another blanket, she went to the window and looked down at the young couple walking in the moonlight, their heads close together, their hands entwined.

Rosie thought of what she had done and wondered how any good Amish man would be interested in a woman who had given herself to the wrong man and in the wrong way. Ezra deserved better. He deserved an Amish woman who would be a support and stand at his side, a helpmate through life of whom he could be proud.

She turned to go downstairs, heavyhearted, knowing she was not that woman.

* * *

Maybe it was seeing John at the door, acting nervous and embarrassed as he asked to take Susan to the singing that softened Ezra's heart. Or perhaps it was his sister's look of concern, as if she thought Ezra would not agree to let her go, that made him review the last sixteen months since their parents had died. He had been too hard on all of them in the beginning. He had been even harder on himself.

Thankfully, he was beginning to realize that Susan needed to be free to find her way in life. She was a beautiful woman, strong in her faith and committed to the Amish way. She would not wander off, seeking the world, as her brother had done.

And Rosie. His heart ached. All Rosie had wanted was to be loved. Anger swelled within him toward her father, who had not provided the positive role model she had needed. If he had been a better father, Rosie would have been content with her life and would have found love the normal Amish way.

Ezra would have continued to watch from a distance as a good Amish man courted her and the banns of marriage were read and the ceremony performed on a Tuesday or Thursday after fall harvest.

Perhaps things happened for a reason, even difficult things that caused pain. The journey to this moment for both of them had been filled with twists and turns that neither of them would have expected, yet they were together now, and if he could judge by what had happened in the barn and the feelings that had passed between them, something good was drawing them together.

Light footfalls on the stairs signaled Rosie was returning to the first floor. He stood, wanting to welcome her, if not into his arms, at least into the kitchen, where they would share coffee and spend time alone together.

He had not expected to be so overwhelmed with her beauty as she came into view. She had lost her *kapp* on the path, and her hair fell softly over her shoulders, encircling her pretty face and big blue eyes, which stared at him full of questions. Did he notice a hint of longing in her gaze, as if she was feeling the churn of confusion just as he was?

He took her hand and drew her next to him. She looked up expectantly.

The guilt lifted from his shoulders. He forgot children were sleeping upstairs, and his sister was saying goodbye to John outside. All he could think about was Rosie and the way she had felt earlier in his arms. Her soft skin, her sweet smell, the way his body responded to her nearness.

He stepped closer and put his hand around her slender waist. The warmth of her touched a place of pain that he had carried too long. He saw her face. Her lips lifted up to his and the world stopped. Time stood still and she was the only thing his eyes could see or ever wanted to see as he lowered his lips and—

"Ezra?" Susan's voice called as she shut the front door behind her and ran to the kitchen. "Did you tell John to ask me to the singing?"

She stopped short when she entered the kitchen. Rosie had a look of shock on her face and he felt equally as surprised. Susan appeared confused as she glanced at both of them.

"Is something wrong?" she asked.

"No, everything is fine," Rosie soothed, stepping farther away from him. "I was just saying good-night."

All too abruptly, she turned and fled up the stairs, leaving him with a jumble of emotions and a yearning so strong it was painful. He had almost kissed her. Their lips had almost touched before Susan, his sweet unsuspecting sister, had interrupted their moment together.

He tried to smile, but he kept thinking of Rosie, who once again was running away from him.

She deserved better than a man with a past, a man who had made too many mistakes to count and who continued to fall short of the mark.

Love was not in Ezra's future. Not now. Not ever.

FIFTEEN

Rosie woke early the next morning. She dressed quickly and got Joseph ready for breakfast. Once downstairs, she placed him in the high chair and cut up small portions of a banana for him to eat as she helped Susan with the breakfast.

Mary ran in with a basket of fresh eggs from the henhouse. She squealed when she saw Joseph and dropped a kiss on his cheek.

"Can I stay and feed Joseph this morning?"

Susan raised her eyebrows. "You know Ezra needs you in the barn."

"Oh, Susan, tell him I am growing so big and am needed in the kitchen."

Rosie smiled and waited until Susan nodded her agreement. "Perhaps Rosie will tell him."

She detected a sly smile on Susan's face as Rosie grabbed her cape. "I will let your brother know that I need your help, Mary. But I think Joseph is too interested in his new friend to feel like eating. Offer him the cup, Mary. He may want a drink of water."

The girl slid into the chair next to him and began to explain everything that was happening in the barn as she lifted the sippy cup to his lips. "When you grow to be a big boy you will help in the barn, too, and you will be able to milk the cows and feed the chickens."

Rosie laughed as she hurried from the house and searched for Ezra. He was standing near the fence, filling one of the troughs with feed.

He looked up, his face full of longing. Her heart nearly broke through her ribs. His look took her back to last night and their almost-kiss. Was Susan's interruption a blessing or not?

Rosie did not know her own heart, and she was totally confused by the mixed messages she kept getting from Ezra.

"Mary would like to help in the kitchen this morning," she told him. "If you can spare her."

Ezra laughed. "She wants to be with her buddy Joseph. He is all she has talked about since she woke this morning. Yes, of course, she can remain in the kitchen."

"I am sorry that we are taking her from her chores."

"But she will help you with Joseph and that is how girls learn to be good wives and mothers. It is not a problem, Rosie."

She nodded, wishing he would say something else, but he turned back to the feed as if he had nothing more to say to her. Nothing about last night or the moments in the barn or whether his lips had touched her forehead.

There she was again, totally confused and not able to decide what he thought of her or if he even thought of her at all.

She turned to go inside, but he called her name.

She stopped and glanced back, not knowing what to expect.

"Your ankle is better?" he asked.

She nodded. "Much better. Thank you."

Rosie hurried inside and was welcomed by Joseph's laughter and Mary's giggles.

Susan smiled. "I am not sure if breakfast is being eaten or played with."

"He certainly is taken with Mary." Seeing the basket of eggs Mary had brought from the chicken coop, Rosie offered, "If you are scrambling eggs, I could break them and get them ready."

"I would appreciate your help."

Working quickly, Rosie broke the eggs into a bowl, added salt and pepper, stirred them with a fork and added a dollop of milk.

Susan stepped closer. "I do not add milk."

"I am sorry. I should have asked before I added it."

"Oh, no, I am glad to learn something new. I cook like my *mamm,* but that does not mean there are no other things to learn."

"According to my mother, adding milk made the eggs smoother." She took the bowl to the stove. "Shall I use the big iron skillet?"

"Yes, please, but let me add butter first."

Once the butter had melted, Rosie poured in the eggs and stirred them as they cooked.

Oatmeal simmered on a back burner, and biscuits baked in the oven. When Susan pulled them out, the rich smell filled the kitchen. "It is good to have a warm breakfast on a cold December morning."

"Christmas will be soon," Mary said from the table. "After school, can we make a pretty chain with colored paper?"

"May we," Susan said, correcting her.

"*Yah*, may we?"

"I am not certain Ezra wants any Christmas decorations in the house this year."

"But we have the paper, and I can make the glue with flour and water."

"I will talk to your brother. Now run to the door and ring the bell." Susan glanced at the skillet. "The eggs are almost ready, and the biscuits are hot. Everyone must eat before school."

"I will return in a minute," the girl told Joseph. "Listen for the bell."

The baby's eyes widened as if he understood Mary's comment. When the bell rang, he kicked his feet and laughed. Mary hurried back to sit at the table next to him.

"Wash your hands, Miss Mary, and pour milk for you and David."

The child complied with what her sister had requested.

Rosie watched Ezra through the window as he added fresh water to the troughs before washing his hands at the pump. The other children did likewise and then followed him inside.

The fresh morning air circled around them, their cheeks ruddy from the cold. As Ezra shrugged out of his coat, she could not help but notice how his shirt pulled over his muscular chest, which brought more thoughts of being in his arms.

Rosie's cheeks warmed and she lowered her gaze, hoping to free her mind of anything except the breakfast needing to be served.

Once the eggs were plated and the plates and bowls of oatmeal placed in front of each hungry person at the table, she slipped into the chair next to Joseph and across from Ezra. With a downcast gaze, she silently gave thanks for this family and for the welcome and love she felt here.

She glanced up and found Ezra starting at her as if he had read her mind when she had focused on love. They both reached for their coffee cups and sipped simultaneously. Again, their eyes met.

Rosie no longer wanted to eat. She took a spoonful of oatmeal and offered it to Joseph, who gobbled it down, followed by another and another after that.

He glanced at Mary between bites. She smiled at him and then at Rosie as she ate. "I like your eggs," she said sweetly.

Susan nodded in agreement. "Rosie's eggs taste *gut* to me as well, Mary. It is the milk she adds. When you help me fix breakfast, we will try her breakfast tip, *yah*?"

"*Yah.*" Mary nodded. "I want Rosie to stay and fix eggs for us every day." She patted the baby's chubby hand. "I want Joseph to stay, too."

"You have all been very thoughtful and have made us feel welcome," Rosie said, carefully choosing her words. "Joseph and I thank you for this."

"It sounds as if you plan to leave us," Ezra said, his brow raised.

She did not understand his comment. Did he think they would stay forever? "*Yah*, we must leave soon."

"How soon?" Belinda asked.

"I am not sure." Rosie fed more oatmeal to the baby.

"You mentioned a cabin," Ezra said from across the table. "There are fishing cabins around the lake area. Perhaps we could go there today."

"Is this wise?" Both of them were cautious of what they said around the children, but there was no doubt that Ezra was talking about the cabin Rosie had visited with William.

"A number of cabins are located on this side of the lake," Aaron said. "Caleb, my friend who likes to fish, goes there often. He noticed a cabin in the woods that had shipping carts piled up on the street for the garbage man to take. The boxes were addressed to the pharmacy in town so he told Peter."

"Peter Overholt?" Ezra asked.

"*Yah.* You know Peter. He lives on the farm at the outskirts of town. You went to school with his brother, Jonas."

Ezra nodded. "What does Peter have to do with the pharmacy?"

"He works there. At least he did. Rayleen is the new pharmacist in town. She bought Mountain Pharmacy a few months ago and hired him shortly after that, but now she told him not to come to work. Peter does not know when he will be needed again."

Ezra glanced at Rosie, and from the look of concern on his face, she felt sure his thoughts were not on their near-kiss or being in each other's arms. The thought that came to her was why Peter was not wanted at the pharmacy. Did the pharmacist have something she wanted kept secret from the teen?

Ezra looked at the wall clock. "David, you and Mary need to leave for school. Finish your milk and take your dishes to the sink."

Both children did as their brother requested. Mary rinsed the plates and stacked them on the counter.

"It is my turn to wash the breakfast dishes," she announced.

"Go on, Mary," Susan insisted. "Ezra is right, we

stayed too long at breakfast. You and David must get on your outerwear. Your lunches are on the counter. Tell your teacher you are sorry if you arrive late."

"I will tell her we have company."

Mary's comment troubled Rosie. "It might be better to not mention that we are staying here."

"Is it a secret?" the little girl asked.

Rosie nodded.

With a knowing smile, Mary brushed Joseph's hair back from his forehead and kissed his cheek. "It will be our Christmas secret."

After the youngest two children left the house, Aaron and Belinda went outside to complete their morning chores while Susan busied herself at the sink and Rosie washed Joseph's hands and face with a warm washrag.

Ezra finished the last of his coffee and then pushed back from the table. "Come with me to the lake, Rosie. We will try to find the cabin you visited as well as the cabin Caleb told Peter about. Like Caleb, I question why the shipping boxes would be at an isolated cabin. Perhaps it is the same cabin you visited."

"It would be hard to know where to look, Ezra. Plus, I do not want to see Larry Wagner again."

"This is not who I want to see, either. We will take the bigger buggy with three rows of seats. You can sit in the rear. With your black bonnet, he will not notice you."

Rosie hoped Ezra was right because deep down she wanted to go with him. Not only to find the cabin that might have clues as to what was happening in town but also to determine if William had been involved in the drug operation. She had been so wrong about him. Rosie glanced again at Ezra, a *gut* man who needed a *gut* woman in his life.

Perhaps it was fortunate Susan had interrupted them before they kissed. Rosie did not deserve Ezra, yet she had wanted him to kiss her yesterday. She wanted Ezra to kiss her today as well.

"We will take another back road," Ezra said as he helped Rosie climb into the rear of the buggy.

"You have many back roads on this mountain."

He laughed. "A man likes to have various ways to travel. This road will take us over the mountain instead of heading back down to the valley, the way we normally go to town. Eventually we will arrive at the lake."

"I do not recall seeing a lake when I went to the cabin with Will."

"Did you see anyone else when you were there?"

She thought for a moment. "I went with William only twice and each time I remained in his truck and saw no one. Will said he had to pick up a package, although both times he returned from the cabin with more than one box in hand."

"Cardboard boxes?"

"*Yah*, each box was marked with a name and address."

"Did you go with him when he made the deliveries?"

"Only once when he made a delivery to Atlanta."

"Do you remember the address?"

She shook her head. "The house was north of the city. That is all I remember."

"What about the cabin, Rosie? Was there anything to help identify it?"

"It was an A-frame and had a screened-in side porch."

"We will search for just such a place."

Rosie pulled her cape tight around her neck. The sun was shining, but the day was cold. Ezra wrapped a heavy blanket around her legs before he climbed into the front seat.

"If a car passes, duck down so they will not know you are there."

"I am not worried," she assured him.

Ezra was. Not overly, but he was concerned and hoping the man in the SUV would remain in town or wherever he lived and not venture to the lake.

Susan stepped onto the porch, carrying Joseph in her arms.

"Keep watch," Ezra told her. "Lock the door while you are home alone and do not let the children linger outside when they come home from school. I have already warned Belinda and Aaron."

"You are worried for our safety?"

"I am worried someone may come here looking for Rosie. Do not open the door to anyone except our family. The man who drives a white SUV is not to be trusted."

"Joseph and I will stay inside with the doors locked."

"That is *gut*."

Ezra nodded farewell and then flicked the reins. The mare snorted as she turned onto the paved roadway.

"You are warm enough?" Ezra asked, glancing back to where Rosie sat bundled under the heavy covering.

"*Yah*, I am fine."

The clip-clop of the horse's hooves and the rumble of the buggy wheels over the pavement made conversation difficult. Ezra wished Rosie was sitting next to him so he could put his arm around her to keep her warm.

The turnoff to the lake appeared. He pulled on the reins. The mare stepped into the turn and increased her pace to a sprightly trot.

"The lake is in the distance. Thankfully we have the road to ourselves." Ezra glanced back.

Rosie smiled. He wanted her to sit next to him even more.

The road ambled downward toward the water, where ducks floated and geese honked as they flew overhead. Today, the lake was devoid of boats and fishermen on the shore, and in spite of the cold temperature, Ezra appreciated the beauty of the rolling hills surrounding the shimmering water.

He stopped the buggy to admire the setting and heard Rosie stir. She climbed from the rear, scooted next to him and inhaled the mountain air.

"It is beautiful here," she said. "I do not remember seeing anything this serene when I was with William. Although perhaps I was not looking at the surrounding scenery."

Ezra's heart faltered. Rosie's attention had, no doubt, been on Will. Tall and muscular and with his wavy hair and thick neck, he'd attracted women, and Rosie in particular. All Ezra could remember was the anger that flashed from Will's eyes and the smirk on his full lips.

"When in love, we do not always see clearly," Ezra said.

She angled her head and looked quizzically at him as if she did not understand the comment. Perhaps she thought he was revealing his own heart. If so, the frown she wore was message enough that she was not interested in Ezra.

SIXTEEN

"A road angles away from the lake," Ezra said as he and Rosie sat on the side of the road in the buggy. "And another road beyond that."

Rosie followed his gaze. "I wish I could remember some landmark that would make it easier to find the cabin."

"Perhaps you should sit in the second seat, directly behind me, instead of all the way in the back. You will be better able to see the landscape and any buildings we pass."

"And if a car approaches, I will hide in the rear."

Once Rosie was settled, Ezra flicked the reins. They turned onto the first road and paused momentarily at each cottage and cabin to give Rosie time to determine if anything looked familiar.

"Do not get discouraged," he said when the road came to a dead end. Ezra guided Bessie to an adjoining side street. At the next intersection, they turned right, heading back to the lake on the second road.

Rosie placed her hand on Ezra's shoulders and leaned forward. "We both hope the cabin will provide information about the drug operation. But what if we do not find the cabin?"

"We will keep looking until we do find it."

His optimism plummeted as their search stretched on. Rosie mentioned never having noticed the lake when she and Will had stopped at the cabin. Perhaps Ezra was wasting his time and hers, looking for something that could not be found. At least not around the lake.

"Aaron's friend saw shipping boxes outside the cabin addressed to the pharmacy," Ezra mused aloud. "Does that mean the pharmacist is involved?"

"She would have to be suspicious with so many patients being prescribed pain medication," Rosie said. "What about Dr. Manny, who treats the nursing-home patients? Would he not be involved since he writes the prescriptions?"

"Perhaps he gets a bonus for the number of prescriptions he writes. Surely some state-wide agency monitors drug prescriptions, yet with so many pharmacies, it might take time to identify abuse."

"Ezra, stop the buggy." Rosie pointed to the right. "There. That is the cabin."

Just as she had mentioned earlier, the small, single story structure was an A-frame with a screened side porch.

"I do not want the buggy to be seen in front of the cabin," Ezra cautioned. "We will look farther for a back path where we can tie Bessie."

"Then we will peer through the windows?" she asked.

"*Yah.* If we want Wagner arrested, we need evidence of wrongdoing. As we both know, the police are often not interested in what the Amish have to say. We will ensure they are interested by providing evidence they cannot ignore."

They rode past the cabin and soon found a path that

angled into the woods. The dirt road was narrow and the buggy bounced over the rough terrain. When they were a far enough distance from the road so they could not be seen, Ezra pulled up on the reins. He hopped down and hitched Bessie to a nearby tree, then he helped Rosie to the ground.

"We must be careful," Ezra insisted. "The cabin appears empty, but this might not be the case. Perhaps you should stay here while I look around."

She shook her head. "I will go with you. I need to ensure it is the same cabin I remember."

"Then we will go together, but if we see anything suspect, we will turn around and come back to the buggy. On this we can agree?" he asked.

"*Yah*, cross my heart."

He wanted to laugh at the expression Mary sometimes used, but they did not have time for frivolity or lightheartedness.

If there was trouble, Rosie needed to flee as quickly as possible. The fact that she would be vulnerable worried Ezra. What they might find worried him even more.

They started to walk, pushing back the long branches and prickly vines. Both of them were silent as they made their way through the underbrush until they arrived at the wooded area behind the cabin.

Ezra watched for movement, then slowly edged toward the cabin. Rosie followed close behind him.

They climbed the steps to the back porch. Ezra held his finger to his lips and stepped to the window. He placed his hands around his eyes and peered inside, grateful that the blind was only partially closed. He could make out a large worktable and folding chairs.

"Boxes are strewn in the far corner, overflowing from

a trash container," Ezra said as he continued to stare through the window.

"Did you try the door?" Rosie stepped closer and grabbed the knob. The door pushed open.

She raised her brow. "For criminals, they are not very smart to leave a door unlocked."

He glanced behind them and to the right and left. "Stay here, Rosie. I will look inside."

Ignoring his warning, she entered the cabin.

His pulse raced. "Someone could be sleeping."

She shook her head. "I can see into the bedroom. The bed is unoccupied."

Ezra followed her. Once inside, he hurried to the table littered with bubble-wrapped pill containers and prescription bottles, and read the names on the labels. "Tom Rogers. Brian Holmes. Annalise Carter."

"Annalise lives at Shady Manor. The pill holders are called blister packs, according to what Nan told me."

Rosie peered at the blister packs in the trash can. "I recognize a number of patients' names."

A car sounded outside. Ezra glanced through the front window. A white SUV turned into the drive. A second car parked directly behind the SUV.

"That is O'Donnell, the manager of Shady Manor," Rosie whispered as her former boss stepped from his car.

Ezra grabbed her arm. "Come. We must leave now."

They hurried to the back door, pulled it open and closed it quietly behind them just as the front door opened.

Heart pounding and with a warning voice chastising him for putting Rosie in danger again, Ezra ushered her across the clearing and back to the wooded area. He glanced over his shoulder, fearing they were being followed.

"Do not stop, Ezra, or they might see us."

He grabbed Rosie's hand, and together they made their way to the buggy. She hid in the rear and Ezra climbed onto the front seat. He slapped the reins and turned the mare toward the road, only this time they headed for the lake, never passing the house again. Ezra needed to get away from the cabin, away from the lake and especially away from the two men involved in the drug racket.

They had found the cabin but had failed to retrieve evidence that would bring Wagner and O'Donnell to justice.

Rosie nudged Ezra's shoulder with something she was holding in her outstretched hand.

"I took one of the blister packs labeled for a Shady Manor patient," she said when he glanced back. "Perhaps it will convince law enforcement to investigate."

As enthused as Rosie seemed, Ezra was less confident. Pill packages would do little to prove what was really happening, even if it had been retrieved from an isolated cabin in the woods.

Without hard evidence to incriminate O'Donnell and Wagner, Rosie would remain one of law enforcement's prime suspects, especially if she was caught with one of the empty pill packs on her person.

Perhaps Peter could provide information about the pharmacist. Was Rayleen involved? If only Peter would be able to tell them.

"Where does Peter live?" Rosie asked after Ezra told her his plan.

"Just outside town. Remember Aaron mentioned his older brother. Did you know Jonas?"

Rosie shook her head. "If he was a few years older

than you, he would have been five or six years older than me. I was a quiet child that stayed to myself."

"I remember you as having your hand in the air, always ready to answer questions and always having the right answer."

She smiled. "Perhaps your memory is mistaken."

"If Wagner and O'Donnell remain at the cabin sorting through their pills, we can drive to Peter's house and talk to him, if he is home. Then we can return to the mountain without running into anyone who could do us harm."

They rode in silence until the town appeared in the distance. Ezra pulled onto a small farm and stopped near the two-story Amish house. He waved to Peter, who peered from the barn.

Ezra met him there. Rosie stayed in the buggy. She needed to remain out of sight, plus, Peter might be more apt to talk to Ezra without her standing close by.

The conversation did not take long. Ezra returned to the buggy and hurried the mare onto the roadway. "We'll take the back way as soon as we come to the turnoff."

Once they were on the mountain path and hidden from view by the dense wooden area that flanked the road, Rosie climbed to the front and slipped onto the seat next to Ezra.

"What did Peter say?" she asked.

"He does not know why Rayleen told him she did not need him at work. Peter said a big shipment had just arrived from one of the pharmaceutical companies. Usually Rayleen has Peter unload the medication while she organizes it on the shelves in the pharmacy."

"What about the opioid drugs that could be sold for profit?" she asked.

"Many of those are kept locked up. Peter does not have access."

"But he sees the meds?"

"He knows where they are kept, but he has no idea how many are in stock. He did check the computer inventory. The pills that came in one morning were disbursed by afternoon."

"To the various nursing homes in the area?"

"Or somewhere else. He saw pills for one of the patients that had not been packaged along with the other medication going to the nursing home."

"What happened?"

"Peter pointed out the problem to Rayleen, but she did not seem concerned."

"What about Nan? Did he see her at the pharmacy?"

"A woman with red hair stopped in two days ago. Rayleen told Peter to go the deli and order his lunch. When he said it was too early in the day, Rayleen gave him twenty dollars for a pizza and told him to keep the change."

"Did he go?"

"He did and when he finished the pizza and returned to the pharmacy, the red-haired woman was gone and Rayleen was on the phone. He heard her say something about a nurse from Shady Manor, but he could not make out what else was being said. Later that day, Rayleen said she no longer needed his help."

Rosie was the reason Nan had visited the pharmacist. Once Rayleen realized the nurse was onto her or onto the nursing-home racket, she must have warned Larry Wagner and the nursing home manager. Had they killed Nan, making it seem like an overdose?

The nurse's death was Rosie's fault. Another mistake she had made that had led to pain and suffering and murder.

Rosie had to leave the mountain. She had to leave so no more people would die. She glanced at the Amish man who had done so much to ensure she remained safe.

More than anything she wanted Ezra to remain safe. She had to leave the mountain not only for her own good and the good of her child, but also for Ezra. No matter how much she wanted to stay.

SEVENTEEN

Mary ran into the house when she came home from school, her face flushed and eyes wide. She stopped in the kitchen and peered into the living area. "Where is Joseph?"

"Upstairs. He is taking a long nap today." Ezra looked out the kitchen window. "Where is your brother?"

"Davey is walking slowly. I ran home because I have to tell Rosie the news."

"Here I am." Rosie came down the stairs carrying Joseph, who rubbed his eyes and looked like he wanted to go back to sleep. When he spied Mary, he started to laugh.

"I need to tell you about the Christmas pageant at school."

Rosie nodded to encourage the girl to continue.

"Mrs. Trochman's baby was to be the infant Jesus, but the family is going to Pennsylvania to visit relatives. Now they must leave early so that means we need a new baby."

She stopped and looked from Rosie to Ezra.

Ezra smiled. "A new baby?"

"A real live baby," Mary explained. "Our teacher said for us to go home and think of a baby we can borrow."

"You are going to borrow a baby?" he teased.

Mary put her hand on her hip and rolled her blue eyes. "We will *not* borrow a baby because we have Joseph."

"Joseph?" Rosie stepped closer. "Tell me what you are thinking, Mary."

"That Joseph could be our infant Jesus."

Rosie glanced at Ezra as she touched Mary's shoulder. "That is nice of you to consider Joseph for your pageant. You and your family have been so generous to have us in your home, but Joseph and I must leave soon."

Tears swarmed the young girl's eyes. "You cannot leave. Joseph is going to be my brother. I am a good big sister. You said how much he loves me."

Rosie leaned down and rubbed her hand over the girl's cheek. "He does love you very much, Mary. You see how he laughs and waves and kicks his feet when you are close by. He does that because he wants to be your friend."

"Does he want to be my brother?"

"I am sure he would want that, as well, if he could talk, but Joseph and I must move to another area. Perhaps someday we will come back here or you will come to where we live and you will be able to see each other again."

"But I told my teacher that I know a baby who could be the infant Jesus."

"What have I said about making promises you cannot keep, Mary?" Ezra cautioned.

She pouted her lips. "But you promised that we would be happy again and that *Mamm* and *Datt* would be watching out for us and that I would feel their love, but all I feel is sadness. When Rosie and Joseph came here, I thought we could forget what happened and start a new family."

Ezra reached for the child and pulled her into his arms, his own heart feeling the pain she expressed. "We are a family, Mary, and always will be a family. You are a wonderful child and *Mamm* and *Datt* are still in our hearts. That will never change."

"But once Rosie came into our house, you became happier, Ezra. Everything changed for the better. I do not want to go back to the way it was."

He closed his eyes, wishing they could all go back to before the robbery, when his parents were still alive. He would be a different son. He would not make the careless comments that set everything into motion.

Ezra was to blame for his parents' deaths and his sister's pain. Yet they could not go back, and if even if they did, that meant leaving Rosie out of the moment and more than anything he wanted her here, standing in the kitchen, her eyes filled with understanding. Perhaps she, more than anyone else, knew about mistakes.

"Ask Rosie to stay, Ezra." Mary burrowed her face into his shoulder. "Tell her she can join our family."

Ezra wanted to do that, but when he looked at Rosie she turned away from him and walked into the living area with Joseph and stood at the window, staring into the distance. She planned to leave the mountain and leave all of them to make her new life in another place. She did not need a man who had thought only of himself and who could not provide the love and acceptance his family needed.

Rosie helped Susan prepare the evening meal while Joseph sat on the floor. The wooden toys Mary had given him to play with surrounded him, but he seemed less than interested.

"Joseph is not his joyful self," Susan noted as she peeled potatoes.

"He slept a long time today, perhaps it is the tooth." Although Rosie worried it could be something more.

She glanced outside to where the children were working with Ezra. "I thought Mary might come inside to play with Joseph, but she is helping Ezra."

"He has been a good leader for our family," Susan pointed out. "And he showers attention on the younger children. I believe Mary's outburst today was more about her own grief rather than his lack of concern. Plus, she has given her heart to Joseph."

Susan reached for another potato. "Joseph is an adorable baby, and your presence in the house has brought a warmth we have not felt in all this time without our parents."

As much as she appreciated Susan's comment, Rosie knew she and Joseph had done nothing to add to the family unity. Instead, they had brought strife.

"Perhaps it is the time of year," Rosie mused. "Christmas is for family gatherings and celebrations. Those not with us are more deeply missed."

She thought of her own parents. Her *mamm* would cook a plump chicken, prepare stuffing, mashed potatoes and gravy for the meal. Her *datt* would eat silently, hardly noticing *Mamm's* efforts to make the day meaningful.

"When I was young, my father would read from scripture the story of Jesus's birth to begin the day," Rosie continued. "It was a joyous time and a holy day."

"You said in your childhood. Did that change?"

"Everything changed as I grew older. My *datt* turned inward. He would spend all morning on the chores, and he ignored the scripture. I always felt I had hurt him in some way, yet I did not know how. I tried to earn his love and drive away the darkness that had settled over our house."

"Your parents had no more children?"

She shook her head. "A sweet niece lived with us for a while when her mother had a difficult pregnancy and needed bed rest. The little one brought joy to my heart, but even she could not change the pall that seemed to hang over our family."

"The child has returned to her parents?"

Rosie nodded. "The family lives in Ohio. I am hoping they might have room for Joseph and me, at least until I can find my way."

Susan raised an eyebrow. "Would that be Katherine's daughter?"

Rosie nodded. "Do you know Alice?"

"I knew her years ago but have not seen her for some time. Ohio is a long way from Georgia."

"But it is time we leave. All of you have been so kind to take Joseph and me into your home."

"And into our family," Susan added. "Mary is right, you have brought a lightness of heart to Ezra and a joy to all of us. We have the room if you wish to stay."

If only Ezra felt the same.

"All of you need to go on with your lives," Rosie insisted.

"I do not think Ezra feels that way."

"He must look for a wife within the community. With me here, he is not free to make that next step."

Susan placed the pot of peeled potatoes on the stove. "I do not think he needs to search farther."

Her words touched Rosie. If only they were true, but Susan saw through her own eyes and did not realize all that Rosie sensed when she was with Ezra. Plus, Susan had a false picture of Rosie. She did not realize what she had allowed to happen and the pain she had caused her family.

The smell of roasting meat filled the kitchen when Susan opened the oven and placed the large pan of meat on the back of the stove. "The broth from the roast will make good gravy. Thick and rich."

Rosie washed her hands and then picked up Joseph. His forehead felt warm when she tucked him close to her cheek. He laid his head on her shoulder and cuddled closer.

"His tooth must hurt," Susan said.

"He feels like he has a temperature. I will rock him by the fire if you do not need my help."

"Take care of Joseph. Will you have something to eat with us?"

Rosie shook her head. "Maybe later, once the baby is feeling better."

She slipped into the rocker and sat close to the wood-burning stove. The warmth was inviting, and she cuddled Joseph in her arms and softly sang a lullaby he liked.

The children and Ezra came inside and peered at them from the kitchen. They talked amongst themselves in hushed tones as if they, too, were concerned about her child.

Ezra washed his hands, then entered the living area

and peered down at the baby. "Susan said Joseph has a fever."

Rosie nodded. "He feels warm. I was hoping he would fall asleep, but his eyes remain open."

"You must eat."

She shook her head. "Not now. Not until he is better."

"We have medication for fever, but it is not for babies."

"I would fear doing more harm since he is so young."

Ezra nodded. "Do as you think best. I will have Susan save a plate for you."

"Thank you, Ezra." The man was thoughtful and considerate, for which she was grateful. If only he could find a good woman to help him take care of the children and be his partner for life.

Rosie glanced at where he stood in the kitchen. Their eyes met and a warmth settled over her. She looked away, forcing herself to ignore any response on her part to his understanding gaze.

The family spoke little during dinner, and Rosie caught the boys glancing with concern to where she sat. They all appeared worried, just as she was.

Ezra encouraged the four younger children to go to bed early. "With sickness in the house, you all need to get a good night's sleep to ward off the germs."

If one of them got sick because of Joseph, she would be even more upset. *Gott, keep them safe and healthy.*

The house sat quiet as she rocked her baby. Joseph's eyes eventually closed and hers did as well.

Sometime later, she woke with a start. Ezra was sitting in a rocker, staring at her. She adjusted in the seat, feeling embarrassed.

Looking down at Joseph's flushed face and feeling the heat radiating from his little body filled her with fear.

She brought his face up to her cheek, the heat nearly burning her. "His fever is too high"

Ezra rose from the chair. "What can I do?"

"Get a washcloth and towel and a basin of tepid water."

"In here." He motioned her to the bedroom where he slept. "There is a clean towel and cloth on the stand. I'll fill the basin with water."

Rosie laid Joseph on Ezra's bed and removed the blankets from around his hot body. Her hands trembled as she unsnapped his sleeper and pulled his hands and legs free.

Ezra returned with the bowl. He dipped the washcloth in the water, rang it out and handed it to her. She wiped the baby's arms and legs and patted Joseph dry with a towel. Then she repeated the process, wiping his face and stomach. Turning him over, she rubbed the cloth gently over his back.

"This should lower his temperature and cool his body a bit, but I am worried, Ezra."

"There is an urgent-care clinic in town that is open until midnight. We should take him there."

Rosie did not want her baby out in the cold with so high a fever, but he needed medical help. If anything happened to him—

She slipped Joseph back into his sleeper, refusing to dwell on "what if."

"I can hold him while you get what you need for the trip to town," Ezra offered.

Much as she did not want Joseph out of her arms, she needed to get blankets and diapers and a bottle with water for the trip.

Ezra took the baby and instead of being stiff, he cuddled Joseph close and peered down at him with love in his eyes. Rosie's heart almost broke at what she wanted for her child—a good father to shower him with love, to teach him the ways of the farm and of life, to counsel and encourage him as he grew.

She turned and ran upstairs to fetch the items for the trip to town.

Soon ready, she took the baby from Ezra's arms, their hands touching, their eyes meeting, both of them struggling with worry about Joseph's condition.

"I will hitch the buggy," Ezra said. "We need to tell Susan."

"I already did. She is praying."

"I am as well," Ezra said with a nod before he hurried from the house.

Alone in the kitchen, Rosie's heart nearly broke as she glanced down at her precious child, sick with a raging fever. She was helpless to care for him.

Please, Gott, do not take him from me. I could not bear to go on. I promise to leave this area and this wonderful family so they can continue with their lives without my interference.

She sighed. Leaving would be hard, especially leaving Ezra.

EIGHTEEN

The night was pitch-black as Ezra hurried Bessie down the mountain toward town. Rosie sat in the rear, cradling Joseph. Ezra glanced back, seeing only her big eyes wide with worry. He knew her face was pale as death, just as it had been in the kitchen.

He wanted to reach out and touch her hand and offer support, but she did not need his touch when her baby was in her arms. Her only thought was Joseph.

Hopefully, a good doctor would be on duty, one who could examine a small infant and diagnose what was wrong. Ezra shivered thinking of what could happen.

He knew too well that everything could change in the blink of an eye. A robbery, a murder, five children orphaned with only a big brother to care for them.

He shook his head, recalling all the mistakes he had made and regretting each of them. If only *Gott* could forgive him. If only he could forgive himself.

Headlights from farther down the mountain appeared in the distance. Usually the road was void of traffic except an occasional Amish buggy with teens coming home from a singing.

Why would a car be on the road this late at night?

He stomach twisted. He had not seen the man with the streak of white hair since the cabin. Hopefully Wagner was still there counting his illegal pills and the money he had to be raking in, as plentiful as a good fall harvest.

Ezra hated to worry Rosie even more, but she needed to be warned. "A car is coming up the mountain. Surely it will pass by, but be prepared to duck down if the driver pulls to a stop."

"Can you tell if it is an SUV?"

"All I see are the headlights." They were positioned higher than on a sedan, which meant it could be an all-terrain vehicle. Not that he would share the information with Rosie.

He braced himself as the auto drew closer. The headlights blinded him for a moment and spooked Bessie. He steadied the reins to keep the mare in line.

Without warning, the SUV swerved in front of the buggy and screeched to a stop.

Bessie balked but stopped just in time.

The driver rolled down the passenger window and leaned across the console. He raised his voice and shouted to Ezra. "Strange to see an Amish man on the road this late."

Grateful that Wagner had failed to recognize him, Ezra said nothing and hoped Rosie and the baby were out of sight.

"I'm looking for an Amish gal with a baby." The man slurred his words as if he had been drinking.

"I have not seen anyone on the road. You should head back to town. A bear is said to prowl the mountain at night. I have heard stories of him crashing through windshields and causing damage even to the biggest cars."

"You're making that up."

"Am I?"

The man pursed his lips as if considering Ezra's warning before he slipped back to the driver's seat and, using the master controls, rolled up the passenger window. He reversed direction and drove off.

Ezra let out a sigh of relief. He turned to the rear, but saw no one. Where was Rosie?

She climbed out from under the blanket, still holding Joseph. "He will not give up looking for me, Ezra. He thinks I have information that I will turn over to the police. If only I did. We must find a way to stop him."

"He will go home now, Rosie. We will worry about him in the morning. Right now, we need to head for the clinic before it closes."

Ezra turned his gaze back to the road and flicked the reins, hurrying the mare to town, to the doctor and to help for Joseph.

Do not let another person die, Gott, especially a precious baby who has found a place in my heart.

Ezra realized someone else had taken hold of his heart.

Rosie.

The urgent-care clinic was ready to lock its doors for the night when Rosie and Ezra arrived with Joseph. They were quickly ushered into an exam room.

"Do you mind if I stay with you?" Ezra asked after the nurse had left.

"Of course not. I appreciate your support."

She cradled Joseph in her arms. He was still so hot.

A nurse knocked on the partially closed door and pushed it open. "I need to get some information." She pulled up a stool to the laptop computer that sat on a small side table. After punching a few keys, she started to fill in information.

"Do you have access to a phone?" the nurse asked.

"No."

"Address?"

Rosie glanced at Ezra. "We are between homes at the moment."

"Some type of contact information is necessary in case the doctor wants to get in touch with you, ma'am."

"Three fourteen Mountain Road," Ezra volunteered his address.

"Thank you, sir. And the baby's name is Joseph Glick?"

"Yes," Rosie responded.

"When did you or your husband notice the baby not feeling well?" the nurse asked.

Rosie held up her hand. "He is not—"

Ezra's gaze met hers.

Flustered, she ignored the nurse's comment. "Joseph took a longer-than-usual nap this afternoon. Later in the evening, he started to develop a fever and refused to eat. He had no interest in toys or—"

She glanced again at Ezra. "Or his seven-year-old sister, who loves him so much."

"Did you take his temperature?"

"I do not have a thermometer."

The nurse raised her eyebrows. Her questioning gaze made Rosie feel like an irresponsible mother.

"Mrs. Glick, did you give him anything to take down the fever?"

"We had nothing in the house for an eight-month-old."

The nurse clipped a device to Joseph's toe and watched as a number appeared on a small digital screen.

"His oxygen saturation level is 98." She placed a digital thermometer under his arm until it beeped and recorded both results in the computer.

"Axillary temp 103," she said.

The words burned a hole in Rosie's heart. "His temperature is so high. What about his oxygen level?"

"His pulse ox is normal. I'll let the doctor know about his temp." She left the room.

Rosie wiped her hand over Joseph's hot brow. "Surely they will give him something to take down the fever," she whispered to Ezra.

"The doctor will order it, Rosie. A little longer and he will be with us."

The doctor pushed into the room without knocking. "I'm Dr. Philips." His name was embroidered on the pocket of the lab coat, which he wore over scrubs.

"Tell me about your son's symptoms."

Rosie repeated what she had told the nurse. "Usually he is happy and playful. Today, he was too tired to interact with anyone."

The doctor felt Joseph's neck, pressed on his stomach, tested his reflexes and looked into his ears and his throat.

"His throat is red. Some spotting. Could be strep. We'll draw blood for lab work and take a urine specimen. The results will be back tomorrow. One of our nurses will contact you."

He checked the computer. "You folks don't have access to a phone?"

"I can return tomorrow," Ezra volunteered.

"The labs should be back by early morning. We'll give you a copy of the results for the child's medical records."

"What do you think he has?" Rosie asked.

"Looks like strep throat to me. We could do a rapid strep test, but I'll just go ahead and prescribe an antibiotic. We'll swab his throat. Something might grow out in the next twenty-four to forty-eight hours. The nurse will give him Tylenol to take down that fever and start an IV. Joseph is dehydrated. Fluids will help. We'll read his blood smear here and do the preliminary urinalysis before you leave."

Rosie glanced at the wall clock. "I am sure the pharmacy is closed at this time of night. Where can we get the prescription filled?"

"We can fill it here and send you home with the meds. Joseph should be feeling better and no longer contagious in twenty-four hours."

The doctor shook their hands before he left the room. The nurse entered soon thereafter, administered the medication and started the IV.

"You folks make yourselves comfortable." She glanced around the room. "I can bring in another chair."

"That won't be necessary," Ezra assured her. "I can use the computer stool."

Rosie pulled her chair closer to the exam table where Joseph was lying. "You'll feel better as soon as your temperature drops," she said, smiling at her little one.

He reached for the IV tubing. She blocked his hand and then dug in the tote where she had tucked an extra blanket and diapers. She had also brought a toy.

"What is that?" Ezra asked.

"A finger puppet Will gave me soon after I learned I was pregnant. He wanted me to keep it for the baby."

Joseph grabbed the toy and waved it in the air. Distracted when the nurse came back into the room to check the IV, he opened his hand and the toy dropped through his fingers.

Ezra picked it up and studied it more closely once they were alone again. "There's something hard inside the puppet."

"Probably a weight," Rosie mused.

"Which seems strange for a baby's toy. You would not want anything hazardous to hurt Joseph."

Ezra turned over the toy and drew out a small metal object. "This is not a toy, Rosie. It is the cover for a flash drive."

She leaned forward. "I do not understand."

"A flash drive stores information that can be saved from or downloaded to a computer."

He scooted next to the laptop. "Let me show you."

"Why would William want his child to have a flash drive?" Rosie asked.

"We will know more when we determine what the drive contains."

Ezra inserted the flash drive into the USB port, tapped the keyboard and watched as information unfurled across the monitor.

"What do you see?" she asked.

"Records. Names and shipments to various addresses in the surrounding area." He scrolled down further. "Looks like as far away as Atlanta."

"Names and addresses? You mean delivery information? Could it be where Will took the packages?"

"More than likely. Patient names are also listed and the number of pills received from each prescription." Ezra turned to Rosie, his brow raised. "The records are quite thorough."

"Will was worried about someone coming after him. He often told me that he needed protection."

Ezra opened another file. Pictures appeared. "Here is a photograph of the nursing-home manager. Another shows Larry Wagner, the man with the patch of white hair."

Ezra clicked on another file. He pointed to the screen. "Look at this photo."

Two young men, probably in their early twenties, who looked alike and had the same swatch of premature white hair. They stood behind a table loaded with prescription drugs.

Rosie leaned closer. "The men resemble Mr. Wagner."

"They could be his sons. Another person stands behind them."

Ezra enlarged the screen and moved the curser so the man came into view.

Rosie's stomach tightened.

The third man in the photo was someone she knew too well.

The man was Will MacIntosh.

Ezra kept thinking about the pictures on the flash drive. The two men in the photo with the swatches of white hair kept playing through his mind. From their close resemblance, they could be twins.

After his parents' deaths, Ezra had worked hard to keep from thinking about that terrible day, yet tonight, everything kept flooding back to him. He heard the sirens in his head and the words of the person who had come to find him at the bar. "Your parents were shot," the man had said.

Bessie had never traveled so fast. Ezra had taken the

back road and had arrived home moments after the ambulance to find both his parents, lying in pools of blood on the floor of the workshop. His father had been pronounced dead, but his mother was still responsive.

He had pushed past the EMTs, dropped to his knees and reached for her hand. "Forgive me, *Mamm*." He had cried like a child who had gone against his mother's instructions, but his guilt involved more than a child's disrespect. Ezra had led the killers to his parents.

The guilt still hung heavy on his shoulders.

Ezra sighed with regret as they approached the top of the mountain. He glanced back at Rosie, holding Joseph, and then tugged on the reins, guiding Bessie through the gate and past the workshop to the house.

Once the buggy came to a stop, he hurried Rosie inside and helped her settle Joseph in the crib. The baby was less feverish and Rosie's relief was evident, although she appeared exhausted and ready to collapse.

"Rest now," he told her. "We can talk in the morning."

"Sleep can wait, Ezra. There are some things I must explain."

She followed him downstairs to the kitchen and beckoned him to sit while she stood by the table. Once he was seated, she began to speak.

"My father made me feel like I was always doing something for which he was not pleased. William made me feel pretty and smart and nice, at least in the beginning. Only Will's type of love was flawed. He was more interested in himself, which I realized too late."

"This is all in the past, Rosie. You do not need to open old wounds."

"I want you to know what happened, Ezra." She glanced down and clasped her hands together as if in prayer. "We drove all the way to Dahlonega to buy a pregnancy test kit. I did not want anyone here in the Amish community to suspect what I feared was true. A few days later, Will gave me the toy for the baby. By then, I had realized my mistake."

Her eyes were filled with pain when she looked at Ezra. His heart broke for the suffering she had endured.

"Will did not love me," she continued. "He loved the control he had over me. A man with a streak of white hair came after him and killed him. I am certain it was Larry Wagner."

"I am sorry, Rosie." Ezra started to stand. He wanted to go to her and hold her close, but she held up her hand to stop him.

"Someday I will tell Joseph about his father, although I do not know how much I will reveal. But that is in the future and right now, I am concerned about the present. I have brought danger to you and your family and maybe my aunt Katherine, as well as being responsible for Nan's death."

"Rosie, you are innocent of any wrongdoing except of loving the wrong person."

"You are right." She nodded. "William *was* the wrong person. When I saw his picture this evening, I knew I had to tell you."

Ezra stood and took her hand. "The picture explained much to me, as well. My mother was still alive when I arrived home that day. As I kneeled beside her, she clutched my hand, her eyes starting to glaze over. 'Doppelgänger,' she tried to say. '*Weisses haar.*'"

Ezra's heart ached, recalling how she had struggled to make him understand. "The EMTs administered oxygen, but she pushed the mask aside. Raising up ever so slightly, she repeated, 'Doppelgänger, *weisses haar*.' Tonight, when I saw the picture, I understood what she was trying to say. Doppelgänger. Two people who look similar, like twins."

"And white hair?" Rosie asked. "You think she was talking about the men in the picture?"

He nodded. "Twins, each with a streak of white hair."

"Your mother was revealing information about the killers." Rosie's eyes widened. "The day we found out I was pregnant, Will told me he would soon have money so we could leave town and start a new life together."

Tears filled her eyes. "Oh, Ezra, I'm so sorry." She turned toward the stairs.

He grabbed her arm. "Rosie, talk to me."

"Do you not realize what that picture tells me? A third man was involved. That man was Will." She pulled her arm from his hold and ran up the stairs.

Ezra stared after her. Will MacIntosh had killed his parents? Could that be so? A chill settled over him.

He walked outside, needing fresh air and a moment to think about what Rosie had said. He stared into the night, then turned his gaze to his father's workshop. Ezra had locked the door that day and had never gone into it after the police investigation.

Needing to face the past, he retrieved the key. Stepping inside, his gut tightened as he saw the blood stains on the floor. He fisted his hands, then stepped toward the row of buggies. With a little work, a few of them would soon be ready for sale. Aaron was right. Stoltz Buggies could flourish again.

He ran his hand over his father's workbench. His tools—saws and plains, drills and bits, hammers and screws and nails—all neatly in their places, just as they had been the day his parents died.

He peered into the "hole," as he and his father called the propane-run hydraulic lift that lowered buggies from the main floor down to the basement below. A buggy sat on the lower level, partially framed—it was the buggy Ezra was supposed to have been working on that fateful day. Instead, he had been with his so-called friends.

Shame covered him. He had not been able to protect his parents because he was carousing in town. Wanting to gain respect among the *Englischers* who frequented the bar, he had bragged about his father's business and the money it earned.

His gut tightened. The day before the murders, Ezra had mentioned the cash his father kept in his workshop, money the twins had come looking for. Had Will come with them?

Ezra thought again of that day at the bar. He could see the profile of a man sitting near him, who had turned to listen—his eyes sparked with interest—when Ezra talked about the money his father kept on hand. That one statement had led to his parents' deaths.

Realization hit Ezra hard.

The man at the bar had been Will MacIntosh.

NINETEEN

That night, sleep eluded Ezra. Instead, thoughts of Rosie circled through his mind. Not only her internal beauty, but also her pretty face and expressive eyes and the way his heart pounded faster whenever she was near. He thought of her in his arms, their lips almost touching.

He ached thinking of what would never be.

She did not need a man who had bragged about his parents and caused their deaths. Whether Will MacIntosh was a killer made no difference. Ezra's parents would not come back to life, and their wayward eldest child would forever carry the guilt for that terrible day that had changed his life forever.

He rose earlier than usual the next morning, needing to leave the comfort of his bed in order to help Rosie. The least he could do would be to pick up the lab results from the clinic in town.

With quick, sure moves, he saddled Duke and took the back path to town. The air was cold, but Ezra did not concern himself about his own comfort. He thought only of Rosie and her baby.

Once in town, Ezra guided Duke past the nursing home. He glanced at the sign in front of the manor.

Dr. Manny, MD. The physician who ordered all the pain pills and extra medication for the patients. Manny had to be involved.

More than likely there were other criminals stealing drugs from the infirmed who ran larger operations with greater profit. However, for a mountain town with a small population, the doctor and nursing-home manager, along with the man with the streak of white hair, were doing well financially with their simple racket. Prescribe drugs, steal them from the patients and sell them to buyers in distant towns.

The local pharmacist was probably handsomely rewarded for her participation and for turning a blind eye to the illegalities of overprescribing highly addictive opioids. She was being bribed to keep her mouth shut and not alert the authorities.

The operation could have continued indefinitely except for an Amish woman who wanted to ensure her favorite patient had medication he needed for pain. Along with Rosie, thanks needed to be given to a nurse who had uncovered incongruences that did not add up. Nan had died because of what she had found.

Ezra's veins chilled. They had killed Nan. They would kill Rosie too. As soon as he had the lab results and any new medication the doctor ordered for Joseph, Ezra would return home and pack up the entire family for a Christmas holiday visit. His mother's family lived in Tennessee. Surely they would open their homes to them.

From there Ezra would notify the Tennessee authorities, who would pass the information on to the sheriff in Willkommen. Once the guilty were behind bars, Ezra and his family could return to the mountain, along with Rosie and Joseph.

Ezra turned at the third intersection and hurried toward the door of the clinic. Hours of operation—6:00 a.m. until midnight. Ezra had arrived just as it was opening.

After tying his horse to the hitching rail, he hurried inside and stopped at the receptionist's desk.

A woman wearing pink scrubs glanced up. "May I help you?"

"I need to pick up lab results for Joseph Glick."

"Dr. Philips will not be in today, but Dr. Manny is available."

"The doctor from the nursing home?"

She nodded. "That's right. Dr. Manny and Dr. Philips own the urgent-care clinic and share responsibilities. A number of other doctors fill in as well." She glanced down the hall and smiled. "There's Dr. Manny now."

The receptionist explained what Ezra needed and handed the lab results to the doctor. He glanced over the forms.

"The preliminary throat culture shows gram-positive cocci," he explained. "No doubt group-A strep. Ensure the baby takes all the antibiotic. A slightly elevated white count, but nothing to be alarmed about. If anything changes, have the mother bring him back. She and her child are staying with you?"

Ezra did not want the doctor who worked at the nursing home to know Rosie and Joseph's whereabouts. "I can contact the mother and give her the information," Ezra assured the doctor.

Once he had the lab results in hand, he hurried to his horse and headed out of town. At the turnoff to the back road, he glanced over his shoulder. His chest clenched as he spied a dark sedan. The car accelerated.

Ezra clucked his tongue and encouraged Duke, but before they could make the turn, the car swerved, cutting them off and forcing Duke into the ditch. The horse lost his footing on the embankment and fell on his side, hooves flailing in the air.

Ezra was thrown to the ground. Air whooshed from his lungs. He gasped, worried about his horse, but equally worried about the manager of the nursing home, who stepped from his car, gun in hand.

"You've caused enough problems, Stoltz. I'll take care of you. Wagner will take care of your girlfriend."

Rosie jerked awake. Jumping from the bed, she hurried to the crib and touched Joseph's forehead. He was warm, but the fever had dropped significantly.

She would let him sleep while she helped Susan with breakfast, but when she went downstairs the kitchen was empty. Rosie added logs to the kitchen stove and arranged the wood so it caught.

Once the fire took hold, she boiled water for coffee, poured it over the grounds in the aluminum drip coffeemaker and moved the pot to the warming area at the back of the stove.

The smell of the hearty coffee filled the kitchen. She opened a number of drawers, searching for a bus brochure. Finding it in the hutch, she pulled it out and read the schedule.

A bus traveled to Cincinnati, Columbus and Berlin, Ohio, weekly. She ran her fingers along the page, needing to find the departure information.

"Today at 2:00 p.m.," she said to herself. The bus would leave some hours from now. She would need to arrive early to buy her ticket. Joseph could sit on her lap.

She would ask Aaron to drive her to town in the buggy. Not Ezra. Knowing Will could have been involved in his parents' deaths made her too upset to talk to Ezra face-to-face. Instead, she would leave a note, expressing her gratitude for all he had done.

She pulled paper and a pen from the drawer, but tears blurred her eyes as she wrote. Her heart nearly broke as she thought about leaving.

Susan's footsteps overhead signaled the girl was up and would soon be downstairs. Rosie sealed the note in an envelope and wrote Ezra's name on the outside, then placed it on the bookcase in the living area. He would find it tonight when he reached for his Bible before going to bed.

Her hands were shaking as she wiped the tears and focused on pouring a cup of coffee when Susan hurried downstairs, apologizing as she entered the kitchen.

"I must have overslept, which is not something I usually do." Susan tucked a stray strand of hair behind her ear. "How is Joseph?" she asked.

"His temperature is not so high. The antibiotic the doctor gave him must be working."

"I am glad." Susan poured coffee for herself. "I heard Ezra earlier and asked if he wanted breakfast, but he declined the offer. I laid my head down for a few more minutes and just awoke."

"Ezra was up early?" Rosie asked.

Susan nodded. "He wanted to go to town. Something about lab results for Joseph and medicine if the doctor ordered anything new."

Rosie glanced at the barn. The buggy was visible through the open door. "He must have saddled Duke and ridden over the mountain."

"That is the fastest route. Hopefully, he will be back before breakfast is ready."

"The children are doing chores?"

"I am sure they are eager to get everything done. Mary mentioned a final pageant practice this morning before school starts. I think she wants to go early and talk to the teacher."

"Probably about Joseph not being able to participate."

"Perhaps. Last night, she confided that the teacher changed the date of the performance because so many families were leaving to visit relatives. The pageant will be held this evening."

"Tonight?"

"With the concern about Joseph being sick, she and Davey failed to share the change in plans."

Rosie's heart ached, knowing she and Joseph would be on a bus this evening, heading to Ohio.

As if aware of Rosie's upset, Susan paused from cutting slices of ham for breakfast. "Are you worried about the baby's safety?"

Rosie shook her head. "No, but it is time for us to leave the mountain and travel someplace new."

"Then you were serious about leaving, as you mentioned yesterday?" Susan asked.

"It is what I must do."

"And what of us, Rosie? Have you thought how your leaving will hurt the children? It will also hurt Ezra."

"You are a dutiful sister, Susan, who loves her brother, but his interests would be better served by me leaving. As I have mentioned before, Ezra needs to focus on his own life and his own future."

"I agree, but that is why you should stay."

Rosie wrinkled her brow. "What do you mean?"

"I mean that Ezra needs time to determine the direction he should take in the future."

"Exactly. Which is why I need to leave so he has time to decide for himself. Right now, he is worried about my safety and Joseph's. That occupies his thoughts. He needs to be free of us."

"I think more than your safety is playing through his mind."

Susan placed a skillet on the stove and added the ham. She scooped a large wedge of butter into a second skillet and sighed with frustration when she reached for the basket of eggs and found it empty.

"I will gather the eggs," Rosie said.

"It is Mary's job."

"*Yah*, and Mary is helping in other ways. Joseph is still sleeping. If you hear him cry, call me."

Rosie hurried outside. She peered into the barn as she passed, seeing the mare she had ridden to Katherine's house. She still needed to talk to her aunt.

The hens clucked as she entered the chicken house and searched the nests. "We need your eggs for breakfast, you sweet ladies," she cooed. "Your eggs are making the children strong and smart and ready for the new day."

Mary joined her there. "I was going to get the eggs soon, but I had to clean one of the stalls. Thank you for helping me with my chores."

"It is no problem. You have been such a help to me with Joseph."

"Is he still sick?""

"His temperature is down a little, which means he feels better. I am sure he would like to see you once the sleepyhead gets up."

"I will come inside soon."

Rosie took the eggs to the kitchen and stopped short, hearing Joseph's cry.

"He just started," Susan assured her. "Bring him down for breakfast. The food is almost ready."

Rosie washed her hands and then hurried upstairs, relieved to see Joseph's cheeks were not as flushed as last night and his eyes were brighter.

"You are feeling better today," she said, clapping her hands. "*Mamm's* big boy is ready to get up?"

Rosie carried him downstairs.

Susan's glanced up from the stove and smiled. "You look better this morning, Joseph. Perhaps you will have something to eat."

"Let me put him in the high chair. A portion of biscuit and a little water might be a good start. If he is interested in food, I will give him more to eat."

As soon as she placed the food in front of him, the baby reached for the biscuit and cup and could not eat and drink fast enough.

Grateful that he was feeling better, Rosie turned to Susan. "I hate to ask again, but would you mind watching Joseph for a short time this morning? I need to talk to Katherine. I was there the other day, but she was not home."

"You will take the buggy?"

Rosie shook her head. "I would like to saddle Duchess instead. The back path will get me there more quickly. I hope to return before the children leave for school."

"Your leg is better?" Susan asked.

"Much better."

"Of course I will watch Joseph. He is such an easy baby and is so full of love." Susan began to plate the food. "Do not forget the riding pants that are on the dresser in my room."

"You do not mind?" Rosie asked.

"Of course not."

After donning the leggings, Rosie grabbed her cape and hurried outside. Aaron helped her saddle Duchess.

"You will be back soon?" he asked, giving her a hoist onto the mare.

"Before you finish breakfast."

At least she hoped that would prove true.

TWENTY

Ezra fought against the rope wrapped around his hands and legs. The manager of the nursing home had brought him to the cabin and tied him up. Now O'Donnell was frantically gathering pills off the table and shoving them into a suitcase.

"I know about your drug operation," Ezra taunted, hoping to unsettle O'Donnell. "The police have been alerted."

The manager laughed nervously. "Some of the police have known the entire time. They enjoy the extra money they receive by looking in the other direction."

"The pharmacist is onto you."

O'Donnell chuckled again. "You Amish are so unworldly. We couldn't do this without the pharmacist."

"She does not want to be involved with anything illegal. Can you tell from the questions she asks and her concern about how much the operation has grown?"

Ezra hoped a portion of what he said sounded plausible. According to Peter, the pharmacist seemed upset. Surely that had to do with what was occurring and her involvement. Providing just a little doubt could be enough to unnerve O'Donnell completely.

"You didn't talk to Rayleen," he insisted.

"Why do you say that? She fills prescriptions for many of the Amish. We are not blind to what is going on. The nurse, Nan Smith, died because she demanded information, but before you killed her, she had called the police and told them her concerns."

"I don't believe you. I told you the police are in favor of our operation. It serves them well."

"I am not talking about the local police. You are right. Most of them are corrupt. But the sheriff in Willkommen. Do you know him? He is hard-working and honest. He listens to the truth."

"You're lying, Stoltz. You don't remember the day you were in that bar talking about your parents and the money they kept in your father's workshop. I was there. I heard you. You were boasting about how wealthy you were and how special your father was." He laughed. "Only you made everyone there take note."

"Especially the Wagner twins, who killed my parents?" O'Donnell raised his brow. "You know that to be true?"

"So does the sheriff. Tell your friend Larry who works with you that his sons should enjoy their last days before they end up in jail."

"You do not have proof."

"Do I not?"

The manager slammed his fist against the table. "So Will *did* steal information."

"You are jumping to the wrong conclusions." Ezra tried to back step. The last thing he wanted was for O'Donnell to go after Rosie. He glanced at the clock. "The sheriff and his deputies will be here soon."

"Your girlfriend, Rosie, must have the information."

"She received nothing from William. You do not have

to worry about her. Worry more about yourself and what you will tell the authorities when they arrive."

"You Amish were never good at lying." O'Donnell pulled out his phone, tapped in a number and lifted the cell to his ear. "Larry..."

He glanced at Ezra.

"The woman's probably hiding at the Stoltz's house. Manny gave me the address. Three fourteen Mountain Road. You were right all along. If Will stole information, she's got to have it. Don't let her get away." O'Donnell smirked. "After you take care of her, come to the cabin and get rid of her new boyfriend."

He disconnected and pushed another button. "Rayleen, it's Bruce. I've got the pills and the money. Meet me at the interstate. A buyer's waiting for us at the airport in Atlanta. Once we leave the country, the authorities won't be able to touch us."

Ezra's blood chilled. He wanted to scream with rage. His plan to outsmart the criminals had backfired. They knew about the evidence and, even worse, they believed Rosie had it in her keeping.

The thought of what could happen if Wagner found her was too much for Ezra to bear. He had made another mistake, and this time it would cost Rosie her life.

"What will I tell Ezra when he returns home?" Aaron asked Rosie after she had mounted Duchess and grabbed the reins.

"Tell him I needed to warn my aunt about Larry Wagner."

"The man with the white streak of hair?"

She nodded. "When I come back from seeing Katherine, I want you to drive Joseph and me to the bus station."

"You are leaving?"

"*Yah*. While you are in town, you must find Peter. Tell him to contact law enforcement and share what he knows about the pharmacy. Wagner and the manager of Shady Manor are stealing drugs from the patients. Rayleen and Dr. Manny are probably involved."

"The local police will not listen," Aaron said. "They did not help after our parents were killed. Ezra calls them corrupt."

"That is why Peter needs to call the sheriff in Willkommen. He will listen and act on what he hears."

Rosie nudged the horse's flank. "Let's go, girl."

Duchess headed down the hill at a good clip. Thankfully, this time, there were no snakes. The mare remained on the path and Rosie stayed in the saddle.

Nearing Katherine's house, she pulled on the reins. "Whoa, girl."

Rosie slipped to the ground and tied the horse to a tree branch near the old, dilapidated barn, all the while watching for anything that looked suspicious.

The door to the new barn near the house hung open. Rosie peered inside, relieved to see her aunt. Katherine was petite and well-rounded with rosy cheeks and expressive eyes that now looked worried as she hurried to greet Rosie.

"I did not expect your visit, child. Is everything all right?"

"I wish it were. I have been staying with the Stoltz family. There is a vile man with a streak of white hair who seeks to do me harm. I fear he might hurt you, Katherine."

"You must be talking about Larry Wagner."

"You know him?"

Katherine nodded. "*Yah*, but I have not seen him for years."

The look on her aunt's face made Rosie step closer. "Is there something you need to tell me?"

"Why do you mean, dear?"

"Larry knows my parents."

Katherine's eyes widened ever so slightly. "Why, yes, he does."

"How could they get involved with someone like him?"

"You should ask your father."

"*Datt* would never tell me anything about his past. Nor would *Mamm*. Therefore you must tell me."

Katherine nodded knowingly, her eyes filled with understanding. "Your father should have told you long ago, dear, about his past. He left the Amish life in his youth and ran with some wild boys in town. Larry Wagner was one of them."

"And my mother?"

"She was a pretty girl and liked the things Larry bought her."

Confused, Rosie stepped closer. "My mother was involved with Mr. Wagner?"

"Only for a brief time. She eventually came to her senses and realized she did not want to leave the Amish community. Your father was interested in her as well. He and Larry sparred often, each trying to earn your mother's love. When your *datt* promised to remain Amish, your mother made her choice."

"And Larry?"

"Supposedly, he left town heartbroken. He reappeared

some years ago. You must have been twelve or thirteen. You and your *datt* were shopping in town. From what I heard, Larry said something to you that bothered your father."

The man on the street who had wanted to take Rosie's picture.

"You look so much like your mother, I think your father worried that Larry would take you from him."

"That is foolish talk, Katherine."

"Of course it is, but your father always sees himself as the victim. He is right, and everyone else is wrong."

"I was wrong to get involved with Will MacIntosh."

"Do not be so hard on yourself." Katherine touched Rosie's shoulder. "Mistakes happens. We know that. So does your father."

"Perhaps, although *Datt* has not been able to forgive my transgressions."

"Shame on him after all the problems he caused in his youth. Your father has always been quick to point his finger at others, yet he ignores the three fingers pointed back at him. That is why he was always so strict with you, child. He did not want you to make the same mistakes he did. What he did not realize was that by being hard on you, he was forcing you out of the family. You did not find love at home. Of course you would look for it somewhere else."

Katherine's words touched a hole in Rosie's heart. "I take responsibility for my own actions."

"*Yah*, but knowing the reason behind the actions allows us to forgive ourselves as well as those whose lack of compassion set us up to make those mistakes."

"I cannot blame my father."

"Perhaps not, child. But I can. Why do you think he

isolates himself from the church? He knows he was at fault, yet he is not willing to admit his failings as a father. The pain he carries forces him to distance himself from his family and from his community. I worry about your mother. She is a *gut* woman to put up with your father."

"Perhaps when I leave the mountain, he will come back to the church."

Katherine's eyes narrowed. "You are leaving?"

"To make a new start for myself and my son. I had hoped Alice would have room for us at least until I can get a job and find a place to stay."

"I am sure my daughter would love to have you visit, but go only for a short time until Larry Wagner, who seeks to do you harm, is stopped. Then come back, Rosie. There is a *gut* man here who could use a strong, sensible woman like you."

Rosie did not understand.

Katherine took her hand. "You are staying at the Stoltz home, *yah*? Ezra carries much of the burden for his parents' deaths. It is time for him to move beyond the past and embrace the present."

"I did not come here to talk about Ezra. I came to warn you about Mr. Wagner."

"If Larry stops to visit or to create mischief, he will not find me at home. Just now, I was hitching my buggy to visit my husband's sister. She has invited me for Christmas. I have locked the house and am ready to go. But first, let me give you my daughter's address. She and her husband are well-known in Holmes County."

Katherine drew paper and pen from her bag and jotted down the address. "Tell Alice I will visit soon. You being there gives me another reason to make the long trip. Perhaps your mother will come with me."

"That would be wonderful." Rosie hugged her aunt. "Enjoy Christmas, Katherine, and be safe."

She glanced at the valley and her heart lurched, seeing a vehicle on the road below.

"Someone comes." She narrowed her gaze. "It is a white SUV."

Katherine steeled her spine and shoved her chin out with defiance. "I am not afraid of Larry Wagner."

"He will stop at nothing to find me, including hurting you." Rosie grabbed her aunt's arm. "Come with me. You can help with the children."

Katherine hesitated for only a moment and then hurried up the hill with Rosie. She untied Duchess and, using a large boulder as a step stool, hoisted Katherine into the saddle and climbed behind her aunt.

Heart in her throat, Rosie spurred Duchess on. She had to alert the children and get them to safety.

Where was Ezra? Rosie had hoped he would be home by now. But his horse was not in his stall as she jumped to the ground and called to Aaron, who was working in the barn.

"Help Katherine from the saddle, then hitch Bessie to the buggy. You and the children have to leave. Katherine is going with you."

Rosie raced into the house. "Hurry, you must leave now," she called to the children. "Grab your coats and capes."

She lifted Joseph from his high chair and wrapped him in two heavy blankets. "Susan, take him. Take my baby and keep him safe."

Rosie glanced around. "Where is Mary?"

"She is making something for you and Joseph. Aaron said you planned to leave soon."

Rosie raced up the stairs, taking them two at a time. "Mary?"

She found the little girl sitting on the floor of her room, coloring a picture. Her face was blotched as if she had been crying, which broke Rosie's heart.

"You must go with Susan and the others, Mary. It is not safe here."

The girl did not understand. Instead she handed Rosie the picture. It was a drawing of her family with each person's name written under the various figures.

Ezra was the tallest. Mary had made him stand above the others, looking strong, with a wide smile on his face. His arms were wrapped around an Amish woman holding a baby.

"That is you and that is Joseph," the child said, pointing to the woman nestled in Ezra's embrace. "I made you part of our family."

"Oh, Mary, if only that could be, but right now you need to hurry."

She ushered the girl down the stairs, wrapped her in her cape and hurried her outside to climb into the buggy. She sat next to Katherine.

"Rosie, come with us," Mary begged, scooting over to make room on the seat.

"I must stay here."

"But the man is looking for you," Susan warned.

"And if he finds me it will give you more time to get away." She hugged Joseph and kissed his forehead. "*Gott* protect you all. Now hurry. Head north and then take the turnoff for town."

Her heart nearly broke with fear that the children and Aunt Katherine would not be able to escape in time.

Rosie would be the decoy. Her own well-being did not matter if the children and her aunt were kept safe.

Ezra! Her heart lurched. *Dear Gott, keep him safe as well!*

TWENTY-ONE

Rosie ran to the edge of the property, where she could see the car below. Wagner was driving like a maniac, coming much too fast up the mountain road. She could make out his face behind the wheel. If she could see him, he could see her.

His eyes widened. He accelerated even more.

She needed to hide. But where? She ran along the drive and stopped at the entrance to the workshop. Something prompted her to reach for the knob. The door opened. Relieved, she stepped inside, then gasped, seeing the stains on the cement floor that surely marked where the Stoltzes had died.

She closed the door behind her and ran to a row of buggies in various stages of completion. Ezra had probably helped his father build the buggies, yet after his death, the work had never been finished.

Seeing a large, open hole in the flooring, she stepped forward and peered down to where a partially framed buggy sat on a wooden platform. The platform, attached to a hydraulic lift, looked like an elevator of sorts that moved equipment from one floor to another.

Rosie backed away from the steep drop-off, thinking again of the fall she had taken, days earlier. Wagner had shoved her down the ravine; she would not let him shove her down the opening today.

The sound of the car turning onto the drive made her heart pound. Her mouth went dry. She grabbed a wooden mallet off the nearby workbench. The heft of it brought a sense of security—a false sense of security she soon realized. Even with the mallet, she would be no match against Larry Wagner.

Gott, help me.

Needing to hide, she climbed into a buggy that looked ready to sell. The upholstery smelled new. An extra piece of the heavy fabric lay behind the second seat. She crawled under the swatch, just as the workshop door opened and Wagner stepped inside.

Rosie tucked herself into a ball and thought of Ezra. Where was he? Wherever he was, she prayed he was safe.

O'Donnell had tied Ezra's hands and feet, but he had not bound them to the chair. As soon as the nursing-home manager left the cabin and drove off, Ezra rocked forward and stood, balancing on his tied legs. He hopped toward the worktable, his gaze focused on a utility knife with a razor-sharp blade.

Leaning forward, Ezra stretched out his hands until he made contact with the knife and nudged it closer. Once within reach, he grabbed the handle and carefully positioned the blade against the rope wrapped around his wrists. With short strokes, he sawed back and forth through the thick hemp.

He glanced at the wall clock, his heart sinking. Time was passing too quickly. His hands cramped from the awkward position, but he would not give up. Rosie was in danger, and he needed to protect her.

He kept slicing the knife against the rope until, finally, with one last forceful thrust, the binding broke free. Relief swept over him. He bent over, freed his legs and raced for the door. He had to get to Rosie before it was too late.

TWENTY-TWO

Hunkered down in the back of the buggy, Rosie was too scared to cry and terrified that Mr. Wagner would see the buggy shake with her trembling. Thoughts of all the struggle he had caused flooded over her, bringing an unexpected swell of determination to outsmart this man who had brought so much pain to so many.

She gripped the mallet, ready to strike if she was discovered. Violence was not the Amish way but neither was quiet acquiescence in the face of evil. She needed to protect the children and stop this heinous creature who would, most surely, do them harm. The longer he remained in the workshop, intent on finding her, the more time they would have to get away.

Please, Gott, she silently prayed.

Wagner's footsteps sounded on the cement floor. Slowly, steadily, he moved closer. She imagined him peering into each buggy, trying to find her.

"Rosie?" he called, his voice low. "Can you hear me?"

He knew she was in the workshop. Did he hear her heart pounding and her pulse thumping all too loudly?

She refused to think of what he would do to her. She only knew what would happen to the children if he found them. She had to distract Wagner until the children could get to safety.

"Rosie?" He stepped closer.

She bit down on her lip, trying to focus on that discomfort instead of his nearness.

"Ezra's hurt and calling for you," the man taunted. "He needs you, Rosie. I'll take you to him."

Lies!

"You know Ezra is a handsome man," Wagner continued. "He likes you, Rosie. He wants to be with you."

She longed to cover her ears and drown out his voice.

"You're hiding from me, only I don't know why. Surely you're not afraid of me."

He stepped closer, then closer still.

The slightest movement would—

In one fell swoop, he threw back the covering and grabbed her arm.

Rosie screamed.

Wagner tightened his hold. "I've got you now."

The mallet dropped from her hands. Unable to pull free, she kicked and gouged her short fingernails into the palm of his hand.

Rage flared his nostrils. "Where's the information Will gave you?" he demanded. "I need it. Now."

She shook her head and continued to thrash her free hand against his face. Her feet pummeled his chest.

He yanked her from the buggy. She fell onto the cement floor, landing on her side. "Aagh!"

Pain ricocheted across her shoulder and down her spine. She clawed at the cement to get away. He kicked her side. Air whooshed from her lungs. She rolled to her stomach, drew up her legs and started to crawl.

He grabbed her hair and pulled back her head. She

screamed with pain. He loosened his hold, then kicked her again. She collapsed, unable to breathe.

"Where is it? Where's the information?" His face was next to hers. His rancid breath fanned her neck.

"Tell me," he threatened.

"I have…nothing."

He slapped her face. "Don't lie to me."

She rolled against the buggy. "A toy…for the baby. That is all Will gave me."

"Where is it?"

"In the house."

"Take me there."

She tried to stand. Her legs buckled.

He kicked her again.

"No!" she cried.

"Stand up," he demanded.

Glancing down into the nearby hole, she felt her stomach roil. She grabbed the spokes of the buggy wheel and pulled herself upright.

He laughed at her struggle.

Through matted hair, she stared at the evil flashing from his eyes. "You killed Ezra's parents."

He shook his head. "You've got that wrong. My boys killed them. They needed money and wanted to earn it on their own."

"You call murder a way to earn money? You are despicable."

"I told them no one would track them down and no one has. Not until you. Did Will tell you what happened?"

"Was he involved?"

Wagner laughed. "What do you think?"

"Tell me!"

"First, give me the information Will provided, then you can learn the truth about your boyfriend."

"You killed William because he knew too much. He wanted to leave town, to get away from you, but he needed evidence. Did he blackmail you?"

"He thought he was smart, but Will was stupid and easy to kill."

"You have no goodness within you."

He tipped back his head and laughed.

The door at the far end of the shop opened.

Ezra!

Rosie's heart stopped. He had come to save her, but saving her meant putting himself in danger. Tears burned her eyes. She blinked them back, needing a way to distract her assailant.

"You loved my mother," she said, baiting him. "But she wanted nothing to do with you."

"What are you talking about?" Wagner snarled and stepped closer to the drop off. "If Emma had married me, you could have been *my* daughter."

"I thank *Gott* for the father I have," Rosie responded.

He raised up, ready to lunge at her.

"Wagner." Ezra's voice sounded loud and menacing.

Larry startled and turned too quickly. His foot slipped over the edge of the drop off. He flailed his arms, trying to gain his balance, and toppled backward into the pit, his hands thrashing the air, his scream echoing in the workshop. He landed with a thump.

Nausea swept over Rosie, followed by vertigo. She clutched the wheel of the buggy, ready to collapse, but before her legs gave way, Ezra was there, wrapping her in his arms.

"Are you all right?"

She nodded.

"Wait here." He glanced into the pit and hit a large button on a sturdy pipe attached to the floor. Slowly, the dropped platform, carrying Larry Wagner, rose to the first floor and came to a stop.

Ezra grabbed rope and tied Wagner's hands and legs to the nearby support column before hurrying back to Rosie.

"Wagner's alive, and he will come to soon. Where are the children?"

"In the buggy, headed to Peter's house. He will notify the Willkommen sheriff."

"We need to join them there." Ezra wrapped his arm around her shoulder and ushered her out of the workshop and toward the barn.

"Are you sure you are okay?" He touched her hands, her arms. He ran his fingers over her back.

Tears streamed from her eyes.

"Talk to me, Rosie. Where are you hurt?"

She was in shock, and suddenly unable to speak. All she could do was step into Ezra's embrace. He held her tight as she cried. Her tears were for all that had happened since she had first fallen in love with Will. For her mistake that caused so much pain to her parents and to Will and to Ezra's parents.

"Rosie, it is over. Larry Wagner will not hurt you again. The manager of the nursing home is on his way out of town with the pharmacist, but they will be found."

"Too much has happened, Ezra."

"What do you mean?"

"I cannot stay," she gasped, knowing they had no future.

"You have to, Rosie. You and Joseph."

"Every time you look at my son you will think of his father, one of the men who killed your parents."

"My mother said, 'Doppelgänger,' that means two people."

"But there could have been someone else, namely Will."

"He may have overheard me bragging about the money my father kept in his shop, but other people were within earshot that day, including your boss at the nursing home. O'Donnell could have shared the information with the twins."

"You are trying to make me feel better."

"I want you to stay, Rosie. My parents died sixteen months ago." He provided the exact date. "My life changed that day, but when you—"

Rosie gulped in a deep breath. "Are you sure of the date?"

"*Yah*, of course, I am sure of this."

"That was the day Will drove me to Dahlonega. We found a drug store and I bought the pregnancy kit."

She grabbed his arms. "It was the day I found out I was pregnant. We had a leisurely lunch in town and did not get home until late that evening. That means Will was not involved with the robbery or the murders."

"Rosie, even if he had been involved, that would not have changed the way I feel about you or Joseph."

The sound of an automobile caused them to glance down the hill. Ezra let out a sigh of relief and motioned the car forward. Rosie wiped the tears from her cheeks as the vehicle pull into the driveway.

Willkommen Sheriff's Department was stenciled on the side of the car. Aaron and his friend Peter sat in the passenger seat next to a big guy in uniform behind the wheel.

Ezra squeezed her hand. "Looks like law enforcement has finally arrived."

TWENTY-THREE

Rosie sat in the living area of the Stoltz house later that same day, holding Joseph in her lap, relieved that all the children were home and unharmed. The EMTs had bandaged the cut on her forehead and a bad scrape on her arm. She was sore and bruised, but thankful to be alive.

"We went as fast as we could," David said, his eyes wide, his words tripping one over the other, as he explained the children's escape down the back of the mountain. "Mary was crying, but Katherine told her *Gott* would provide."

"I was scared," the little girl said truthfully. She slipped her hand into Rosie's. "I did not want anything to happen to you."

"You were brave, Mary." Rosie looked at all of them. "You were all very brave."

"We went to Peter's house," Belinda explained. "And stayed with his *mamm* while Aaron and Peter hurried to the grocery and called the Willkommen sheriff's department."

"The pharmacist had already notified them," Aaron added. "Rayleen had let Mr. O'Donnell think she liked him, but all the time she had been gathering evidence on the drug operation. She knew the police in town were corrupt and feared if she did not get outside help, she might end up dead, like the nurse."

"But how did you boys meet up with the sheriff?" Ezra asked.

"We saw his car parked in front of the pharmacy and ran to tell him what was happening on the mountain. He wanted us to show him the way, although he planned to drop us at a neighbor's house. When you waved us forward, Ezra, we knew we would be safe."

"The sheriff's timing was perfect," Ezra said. "And the local police and ambulance arrived soon after the sheriff."

"Did they catch the manager of the nursing home?" Belinda asked.

Ezra nodded. "*Yah*, Mr. O'Donnell was apprehended with a suitcase filled with patient drugs from the nursing home. The staff is being questioned and the FBI has been called in to determine if any drugs crossed state lines. The Wagner twins and Dr. Manny were also arrested, and law enforcement is studying the information Rosie was able to provide on a flash drive."

"What about Mr. Wagner?" David asked.

"He is in the hospital now and expected to recover." Rosie patted the boy's shoulder. "Why do you ask, Davey?"

"Before we dropped your aunt Katherine off at her house, she said she knew him when he was a young man. He made mistakes and did not try to be a good person. She said we should always try to do our best."

Rosie nodded. "Katherine is right. I wish she could have been with us this evening, but she is leaving in the morning to visit her sister and will stay for Christmas."

The children sat in silence for a long moment, each one, no doubt, reflecting on what had happened.

"I give thanks to *Gott* that we are all together." Ezra shared what Rosie was thinking.

Suddenly, he glanced at the wall clock and smiled. "Get your coats and capes, children. We must hurry to the schoolhouse."

Mary looked confused, then her face widened into an excited smile. "The Christmas pageant."

She placed her hand on Joseph's forehead. "He feels cool, Rosie. We still need a baby Jesus."

Rosie laughed. "I think Joseph would like to be in the pageant as long as you will be near him, Mary."

"Did I not tell you?" Her face beamed. "Because my name is Mary, I get to hold Joseph while the angels sing and the shepherds visit the manger scene."

David stuck out his chest. "I am a wise man."

Ezra laughed and ruffled David's hair. "You are wise beyond your years. Now hurry, children, so we can get to school on time."

The schoolhouse was abuzz with activity when Rosie and Ezra found seats. Mary held Joseph and stood near the front of the classroom with a blue veil draped over her blond hair. Joseph was wrapped in a blanket, looking sweet and innocent. David stood to the side with the other two wise men.

Susan had found John Keim in the crowd and was sitting next to him. Belinda was chatting with a girl-friend and Aaron and Peter were surrounded by friends, who probably wanted to hear more about riding in the sheriff's car.

Rosie sighed, relieved that she knew a little more

about Will's involvement with the drug racket. He had attempted to gather evidence to incriminate the guilty, although whether he planned to give the evidence to the authorities or use it as leverage to be free of the operation, she would never know. At least he had not been involved in the robbery and murders.

Ezra placed his hand on her shoulder. She smiled at the warmth of his gaze and the strength of him as his arm touched hers. The teacher snapped her fingers to get the children's attention. The room started to quiet.

"Mary kept her secret about being the star of the pageant," Rosie whispered.

Ezra nodded. "Usually she tells everything, but she kept this a surprise. No wonder she wanted Joseph to be in the pageant."

He leaned closer and winked playfully. "There is a secret I have not told you yet."

Her cheeks warmed. She tilted her head. "Is it a Christmas secret?"

"Hmm. I guess it is."

"Are you going to tell me?"

"Not now." He glanced at the front of the classroom. "The pageant is starting. I will tell you later."

TWENTY-FOUR

That night, after the evening meal had been eaten and the dishes washed and put away, the children went upstairs as if they knew Ezra and Rosie needed time alone.

Susan offered to put Joseph to bed and Rosie appreciated her thoughtfulness.

Ezra took Rosie's hand once they were alone. "Remember the night John Keim came to the door to talk to Susan and you said they would huddle in the cold just to be together?"

She nodded. "I remember."

"If you do not mind, I would prefer we stay inside to talk."

Rosie laughed. "Otherwise the children would be watching us through their bedroom windows."

He squeezed her hand. "I wanted to tell you how much you mean to me, Rosie, and how I need you in my life. So much has happened recently and some people would think that more time would be needed, but I have loved you my whole life."

Her heart nearly burst at his words, the feeling of being loved and accepted filling her to overflowing.

"I love you," he said again. "I have always loved you since I first noticed you in school, only you never had an interest in me, and I never thought I had a chance to win your heart. If not for the mistakes we both made, if not for the pain of losing my parents, I might never have had the courage to tell you how I feel."

"Oh, Ezra, you don't know what you are saying."

"But I do know—I know I love you, and just as Mary said, I want you and Joseph to be part of our family. I want to be Joseph's father and help you raise him. He is wonderful baby, and he will grow into a *gut* man. But I want more children, and we will add onto our house. Aaron and I will run the buggy shop and make good buggies for the community that will bring honor to my father's name. He was not proud of my actions before his death, but he always knew that with *Gott*'s help, I could turn my life around. First, I must be baptized, then…"

"It is too soon for us, Ezra. You do not know what you are saying."

"Rosie, you are a beautiful woman. You make me a better man. I want to spend my life with you forever, if you will have me."

"You are you asking me to marry you?" she asked, unwilling to believe her ears.

He nodded. "If you say no, I will not be able to—"

Raising on tiptoe, she captured his lips with hers, and cuddled more closely against him, both of them melding together. When she finally pulled back, she smiled sweetly.

"My answer is yes." She laughed. "Yes, Ezra Stoltz, I will marry you."

"On Christmas?"

She shook her head. "You know the banns must be announced in church for three weeks. We must prepare the house. The children will help. I will ask Susan to be my attendant. Dresses need to be stitched. I must buy a new *kapp*. Food must be cooked so that everyone will be able to join in our celebration."

"Your parents?"

"*Yah*, I will talk to my *datt* and tell him I understand why he was hard on me. I must forgive him. Then perhaps he will be able to forgive me."

"And I will talk to the bishop about accepting baptism." Ezra pulled her closer. "For so long, I struggled with anger and guilt, but now my heart holds only joy."

His eyes twinkled as he gazed down at her. "We will tell the children after we read the Nativity story on Christmas morn. Until then it will be our Christmas secret."

"I like secrets," she sighed, "when I share them with you."

She turned her face to his. Her heart soared as they kissed, sealing the promise of their future together.

"Merry Christmas, Rosie."

"Merry Christmas, Ezra. You have given me the best gifts of all—the gift of family, the gift of a future walking at your side and, most important, the gift of love."

He brushed his lips against her forehead. "*Gott* rescued us from a place of darkness and brought us into His light."

She nodded. "He has blessed both of us by bringing us together. Forever."

"Which is how long I want to keep kissing you."

Ezra's voice was low and husky with emotion as he lowered his lips to hers.

Forever, she thought, was not nearly long enough.

* * * * *

If you enjoyed this story, look for the other books in the Amish Protectors series:

Amish Refuge
Undercover Amish
Amish Rescue

Dear Reader,

I hope you enjoyed *Amish Christmas Secrets*, Book 4 in my Amish Protectors series (Book 1, *Amish Refuge*; Book 2, *Undercover Amish*; and Book 3, *Amish Rescue*). With nowhere to go, Rosie Glick turns to Ezra Stoltz when the man who killed the father of her child comes after her. Ezra knows Rosie's hiding secrets. But Ezra has secrets of his own. The mistakes they both made during their youthful attraction to the *Englisch* life will haunt them forever, unless they can stop the man who's out to do Rosie harm. If you carry the guilt of past mistakes, I hope Rosie and Ezra's story will lead you to forgiveness and peace.

I pray for my readers each day and would love to hear from you. Email me at debby@debbygiusti.com or write me c/o Love Inspired, 195 Broadway, 24th Floor, New York, NY 10007. Visit me at www.DebbyGiusti.com and at www.Facebook.com/debby.giusti.9.

As always, I thank God for bringing us together through this story.

Wishing you abundant blessings,
Debby

COMING NEXT MONTH FROM
Love Inspired® Suspense

Available November 6, 2018

VALIANT DEFENDER
Military K-9 Unit • by Shirlee McCoy

When Captain Justin Blackwood's teenage daughter is kidnapped by the serial killer he's been hunting, he's desperate to stop the Red Rose Killer from making her his next victim. Can he and Captain Gretchen Hill and their K-9 partners save his daughter and capture a killer?

AMISH CHRISTMAS EMERGENCY
Amish Country Justice • by Dana R. Lynn

Alexa Grant's stalker is determined that if he can't have her, nobody can—even if it means killing her. And as she searches for a safe haven in Amish country, it's Sergeant Gavin Jackson's job to protect Alexa...or risk losing her to a deadly secret admirer.

LOST CHRISTMAS MEMORIES
Gold Country Cowboys • by Dana Mentink

Tracy Wilson witnessed a murder—but after a head injury, she can't remember who it was. Now someone plans to silence her for good, and only cowboy Keegan Thorn believes her. Can she recover her memory in time to save her life?

CHRISTMAS HIDEOUT
McKade Law • by Susan Sleeman

Fleeing from her dangerous ex-boyfriend, single mother Nicole Dyer takes refuge in a cabin on a ranch—and is discovered by the owner, Deputy Matt McKade. When threats escalate to attempts on Nicole's life, Matt is the only one she trusts to keep her and her daughter safe.

DEADLY CHRISTMAS DUTY
Covert Operatives • by Virginia Vaughan

Former navy SEAL Noah Cason turns to prosecutor Melinda Steele for help getting justice for his sister. But when Melinda is attacked, she and her son are the ones who need *his* help. Under Noah's protection, can they stay alive long enough to figure out who wants them dead?

CHRISTMAS UNDER FIRE
Mountie Brotherhood • by Michelle Karl

It's Mountie Aaron Thrace's duty to guard visiting dignitary Cally Roslin during her stay in Canada—but he never expects he'll be facing down ruthless assailants determined that she won't survive the holidays. With danger and a snowstorm closing in, can he make sure she lives to see Christmas?

---

*The final battle with the Red Rose Killer begins when he
kidnaps Captain Justin Blackwood's teenage daughter.*

Read on for a sneak preview of
Valiant Defender *by Shirlee McCoy,*
*the exciting conclusion to the Military K-9 Unit miniseries,
available November 2018 from Love Inspired Suspense.*

Canyon Air Force Base was silent. Houses shuttered,
lights off. Streets quiet. Just the way it should be in the
darkest hours of the morning. Captain Justin Blackwood
didn't let the quiet make him complacent. Seven months
ago, an enemy had infiltrated the base. Boyd Sullivan, aka
the Red Rose Killer—a man who'd murdered five people
in his hometown before he'd been caught—had escaped
from prison and continued his crime spree, murdering
several more people and wreaking havoc on the base.

"What are your thoughts, Captain?" Captain Gretchen
Hill asked as he sped through the quiet community.

"I don't think we're going to find him at the house," he
responded. "But when it comes to Boyd Sullivan, I believe
in checking out every lead."

"The witness reported lights? She didn't actually see
Boyd?"

"She didn't see him, but the family who lived in the
house left for a new post two days ago. Lots of moving

trucks and activity. She's worried Sullivan might have noticed and decided to squat in the empty property."

"Based on how easily Boyd has slipped through our fingers these past few months, I'd say he's too smart to squat in base housing," Gretchen said.

"I agree," Justin responded. He'd been surprised at how much he enjoyed working with Gretchen. He'd expected her presence to feel like a burden, one more person to worry about and protect. But she had razor-sharp intellect and a calm, focused demeanor that had been an asset to the team.

"Even if he decided to spend a few nights in an empty house, why turn on lights?"

"If he's there, he wants us to know it," Justin responded. It was the only explanation that made sense. And it was the kind of game Sullivan liked to play—taunting his intended victims, letting them know that he was closing in.

He needed to be stopped.

Tonight.

For the sake of the people on base and for his daughter Portia's sake.

Don't miss
Valiant Defender *by Shirlee McCoy,*
available November 2018 wherever
Love Inspired® Suspense books and ebooks are sold.

www.LoveInspired.com

Get 4 FREE REWARDS!

We'll send you 2 FREE Books plus 2 FREE Mystery Gifts.

Love Inspired® Suspense books feature Christian characters facing challenges to their faith... and lives.

FREE Value Over **$20**

YES! Please send me 2 FREE Love Inspired® Suspense novels and my 2 FREE mystery gifts (gifts are worth about $10 retail). After receiving them, if I don't wish to receive any more books, I can return the shipping statement marked "cancel." If I don't cancel, I will receive 4 brand-new novels every month and be billed just $5.24 each for the regular-print edition or $5.74 each for the larger-print edition in the U.S., or $5.74 each for the regular-print edition or $6.24 each for the larger-print edition in Canada. That's a savings of at least 13% off the cover price. It's quite a bargain! Shipping and handling is just 50¢ per book in the U.S. and 75¢ per book in Canada*. I understand that accepting the 2 free books and gifts places me under no obligation to buy anything. I can always return a shipment and cancel at any time. The free books and gifts are mine to keep no matter what I decide.

Choose one: ☐ **Love Inspired® Suspense**
Regular-Print
(153/353 IDN GMY5)

☐ **Love Inspired® Suspense**
Larger-Print
(107/307 IDN GMY5)

Name (please print)

Address   Apt. #

City   State/Province   Zip/Postal Code

Mail to the **Reader Service**:
IN U.S.A.: P.O. Box 1341, Buffalo, NY 14240-8531
IN CANADA: P.O. Box 603, Fort Erie, Ontario L2A 5X3

Want to try two free books from another series! Call 1-800-873-8635 or visit www.ReaderService.com.

*Terms and prices subject to change without notice. Prices do not include applicable taxes. Sales tax applicable in N.Y. Canadian residents will be charged applicable taxes. Offer not valid in Quebec. This offer is limited to one order per household. Books received may not be as shown. Not valid for current subscribers to Love Inspired Suspense books. All orders subject to approval. Credit or debit balances in a customer's account(s) may be offset by any other outstanding balance owed by or to the customer. Please allow 4 to 6 weeks for delivery. Offer available while quantities last.

Your Privacy—The Reader Service is committed to protecting your privacy. Our Privacy Policy is available online at www.ReaderService.com or upon request from the Reader Service. We make a portion of our mailing list available to reputable third parties that offer products we believe may interest you. If you prefer that we not exchange your name with third parties, or if you wish to clarify or modify your communication preferences, please visit us at www.ReaderService.com/consumerchoice or write to us at Reader Service Preference Service, P.O. Box 9062, Buffalo, NY 14240-9062. Include your complete name and address.

LIS18

Looking for inspiration in tales
of hope, faith and heartfelt romance?

Check out **Love Inspired**® and
Love Inspired® **Suspense** books!

New books available every month!

CONNECT WITH US AT:

Facebook.com/groups/HarlequinConnection

Facebook.com/HarlequinBooks

Twitter.com/HarlequinBooks

Instagram.com/HarlequinBooks

Pinterest.com/HarlequinBooks

ReaderService.com

Love Inspired®

LIGENRE2018R2

*With her family in danger of being separated,
could marriage to a newcomer in town
keep them together for the holidays?*

Read on for a sneak preview of
An Amish Wife for Christmas *by Patricia Davids,
available in November 2018 from Love Inspired!*

"I've got trouble, Clarabelle."

The cow didn't answer her. Bethany pitched a forkful
of hay to the family's placid brown-and-white Guernsey.
"The bishop has decided to send Ivan to Bird-in-Hand
to live with Onkel Harvey. It's not right. It's not fair. I
can't bear the idea of sending my little brother away. We
belong together."

Clarabelle munched a mouthful of hay as she regarded
Bethany with soulful deep brown eyes.

"Advice is what I need, Clarabelle. The bishop said
Ivan could stay if I had a husband. Someone to discipline
and guide the boy. Any idea where I can get a husband
before Christmas?"

"I doubt your cow has the answers you seek, but if
she does I have a few questions for her about my own
problems," a man said.

Bethany spun around. A stranger stood in the open
barn door. He wore a black Amish hat pulled low on his
forehead and a dark blue woolen coat with the collar
turned up against the cold.

The mirth sparkling in his eyes sent a flush of heat to her cheeks. How humiliating. To be caught talking to a cow about matrimonial prospects made her look ridiculous.

She struggled to hide her embarrassment. "It's rude to eavesdrop on a private conversation."

"I'm not sure talking to a cow qualifies as a private conversation, but I am sorry to intrude."

He didn't look sorry. He looked like he was struggling not to laugh at her.

"I'm Michael Shetler."

She considered not giving him her name. The less he knew to repeat the better.

"I am Bethany Martin," she admitted, hoping she wasn't making a mistake.

"Nice to meet you, Bethany. Once I've had a rest I'll step outside if you want to finish your private conversation." He winked. One corner of his mouth twitched, revealing a dimple in his cheek.

"I'm glad I could supply you with some amusement today."

"It's been a long time since I've had something to smile about."

Inspirational Romance to Warm Your Heart and Soul

Join our social communities to connect with other readers who share your love!

Sign up for the Love Inspired newsletter at **www.LoveInspired.com** to be the first to find out about upcoming titles, special promotions and exclusive content.

CONNECT WITH US AT:

Facebook.com/groups/HarlequinConnection

 Facebook.com/LoveInspiredBooks

 Twitter.com/LoveInspiredBks

LISOCIAL2018